"Zach, the shooter was here!" Janel cried.

Janel yanked her arm away from a nurse trying to calm her, and handed Zach the card.

Reading the threatening message made Zach's blood boil. "Where did you get this?"

She bit her lip as if trying to recall every detail. "I was taking a nap when a man wearing scrubs came in. He gave me the card and left. I thought he was hurrying back to work until I read the words inside." She sucked in a breath. "He might be the shooter."

"You're wrong," the nurse corrected. "You just described one of our orderlies and he's been here all day. I saw him come out of your room. He was halfway down the hall when you screamed and was about to rush back to help you."

"Oh." Janel still sounded afraid. "Then the shooter is out there somewhere...waiting. Watching..."

Tina Wheeler is a retired teacher and award-winning author. She enjoys spending time with her large extended family, brainstorming with writing friends, discovering new restaurants and traveling with her husband. Although she grew up near a desert in Arizona, her favorite place to plot a new story is on a balcony overlooking the ocean.

Books by Tina Wheeler

Love Inspired Suspense

Ranch Under Fire
Ranch Showdown
Ambush on the Ranch

Visit the Author Profile page at LoveInspired.com.

Ambush on the Ranch

TINA WHEELER

LOVE INSPIRED SUSPENSE
INSPIRATIONAL ROMANCE

LOVE INSPIRED® SUSPENSE
INSPIRATIONAL ROMANCE

ISBN-13: 978-1-335-63847-2

Recycling programs for this product may not exist in your area.

Ambush on the Ranch

Love Inspired
22 Adelaide St. West, 41st Floor
Toronto, Ontario M5H 4E3, Canada
www.LoveInspired.com

Printed in Lithuania

MIX
Paper | Supporting responsible forestry
FSC® C021394

I sought the Lord, and he heard me,
and delivered me from all my fears.
—*Psalm* 34:4

To my sister, who is always there
to encourage, advise, chauffeur or offer her
home-improvement skills. Her generosity is boundless.

ONE

Help! God, please help me! Janel Newman dodged one pine tree, then another. Her lungs burned with each breath as she pumped her arms harder, forcing her feet to run faster in the cowgirl boots she hadn't fully broken in yet.

A bullet whizzed over her shoulder, splintering bark off a tree in her path.

Panic struck, and she jolted in a new direction.

Every muscle resisted her effort to move another inch. She ached from head to blistering toes. How much more of a beating could her body take before it failed, leaving her a helpless target?

Racing toward a copse of overgrown bushes, she spotted a boulder barely visible in the dense Northern Arizona forest. When the moment was right, she circled back around the huge rock and crouched as low as her tired, cramping legs would allow. With only enough energy left to breathe, she leaned against the hard granite for support.

Why hadn't she minded her own business?

None of this would have happened if she'd driven straight to work instead of making that U-turn.

The encroaching sound of pounding footsteps warned he was coming closer.

Fear consumed her.

He suddenly stopped, and silence hung heavy in the air. She strained to listen. Where did he go? In her mind, she pictured the murderer scanning his surroundings from beneath his sunglasses.

She pulled her elbows in closer—a desperate attempt to shrink lower behind the boulder, the only thing between her and certain death.

His footfalls started again, and he drew nearer. He was coming straight for her.

Her thumping heart echoed in her ears.

She shoved aside the intense urge to run because he'd shoot the second she stood.

Life. She was choosing to live—if God wanted her opinion on the matter.

The man who wanted her dead stepped even closer.

His shadow fell over the boulder onto a patch of snow inches away from her boots. She froze, afraid to move, to breathe, to even think.

Seconds later, the sound of someone else traveling through the forest carried on the chilly breeze. The shooter's shadow disappeared as he ran in the newcomer's direction.

She waited and waited, then pushed off the rock and sprinted away. Her destination: the trees with the widest trunks, hoping they'd provide protection.

A shot rang out.

The bullet missed, and she continued fleeing as fast as she could. A grunting sound made her glance back long enough to see the shooter trip and fall. Hoping to take advantage of the situation, she fought to quicken her sprint. She had to get away.

Out of the corner of her eye, she thought she saw a horse in the distance. Was she hallucinating? Or did her pursuer have an accomplice coming to join the hunt?

Zach Walker glanced about as he quickly guided his chestnut-colored quarter horse through the dense forest in search of a suspected murderer: a man wearing a black hoodie who'd escaped into the forest seconds after a landscape worker had been shot and killed. Their suspect had a twenty-minute lead, but the sound of two gunshots gave them a general direction to home in on.

The other Mounted Fugitive Retrieval Team members were riding toward that area from different parts of the forest. Zach, a Sedona rancher, was the only fully trained volunteer, sworn in and given a badge. He could perform the same duties as any other county deputy sheriff when needed.

After covering another half mile, Zach pulled

the reins to halt Copper. He pushed back the brim of his hat and listened for sounds of movement. A breeze carried the scent of pine, and the sun's rays filtered through the thick branches of evergreen trees. The signs of a peaceful winter day belied the threat that could strike at any second, around any turn.

Another gunshot fired, and the forest sprang alive with the flapping of wings from birds soaring off their perches. Copper bobbed his head.

"Let's go, boy."

The pair adeptly navigated the terrain with a sense of urgency, closing the gap between them and the shooter. A petite blonde emerged from the shadows fifty feet away. Her presence surprised him. There was no good reason for her to be here.

He was about to yell to her when another shot startled Copper and propelled the woman in a new direction. Zach's pulse raced as he dismounted and secured his horse behind a boulder. He removed his Glock from its holster and peered around the jagged granite concealing his position.

The woman glanced back over her shoulder, and he caught a full view of her face. *Janel? From church?* Was the fugitive trying to shoot her? As he watched, her sweater caught on a branch, and after jerking it free while still trying to run, she smacked into a sturdy tree trunk. She bounced off and collapsed into a heap on the ground.

Zach cringed. He desperately wanted to help

her but couldn't risk moving closer. Not until he'd dealt with the shooter. Suppressing his concern for Janel, he quietly radioed a quick update to his team.

A bullet whizzed through the air, high above her still body.

The sound of boots crunching a pine cone on the forest floor gave away the shooter's location. He must not have detected Zach's and Copper's presence.

Zach needed to draw the man away from Janel before he risked engaging in a confrontation. Coming across a rock the size of an orange, he threw it at a towering pine. The branches swayed, and another shot discharged.

Taking cover behind a bush, he waited for the shooter to step out into the open. The team was working on the premise that this shooter and the fugitive were the same person. Through his radio's earpiece, he heard the team converging on his GPS coordinates. They would be here soon.

Another footfall revealed the shooter's new position. Zach held his weapon tight as he shifted to the other side of the bush to get a better view. All he could see of the man hiding behind a tree was part of a black hoodie and reflective sunglasses... and the pistol he lifted.

Zach identified himself as a sheriff's deputy. "Drop your weapon!"

The fugitive aimed.

Zach fired.

A jerking motion and guttural response told Zach he'd hit his mark—the man's shoulder.

Copper snorted and pranced in place.

Voices in the distance, accompanied by hooves stomping over dirt, sent the man fleeing.

"I see him!" a deputy shouted. "Average height and build, still wearing the hoodie."

"He's heading north," another responded.

Zach rushed back to Janel, keeping an eye out for the shooter in case he tried to sneak up on them. She moaned. A slight utterance, but it signaled she was alive. His breathing relaxed.

"Help's on the way." He crouched and pushed strands of her long hair away from the goose egg growing on her forehead. This was all too surreal. During their many conversations at church, she'd mentioned more than once that she wasn't into hiking or camping, so what was she doing deep in the forest?

Her lids fluttered open, and she stared up at him as she lifted a hand to her head. Her sky blue eyes held no recognition. "Where am I?"

When she tried to sit up, he stopped her. "You might have a concussion."

Zach radioed for medical assistance while continuing to glance about for any sign of danger. From what he heard next through his earpiece, he suspected the fugitive was racing toward the freeway. While the mounted team headed in that direction, the lieutenant gave the all clear for EMTs to move in.

"My head hurts. A lot." Janel closed her eyes again and repeated, "Where am I?"

"You're in the forest near Flagstaff. Do you remember why you're here?"

She gave a small groan. "No. I don't."

"Do you recognize me?" He hoped so. Zach first met Janel six years ago at a fall festival they both spearheaded. He'd been impressed by the Sedona art gallery owner, who had the business connections to secure donations and find vendors. It hadn't taken long for them to develop a casual friendship. She was kind and generous, not to mention beautiful, with her heart-shaped face and flawless complexion. He would have asked her out if she hadn't been dating an instructor at the university in Flagstaff. Was her boyfriend nearby?

Janel peered up at him, her lids partially open. "*Should* I recognize you?"

"We're friends from church." He prayed her memory issues were temporary. The possibility of brain damage worried him. "Try to relax. The medics will be here any minute now."

His gaze shifted to her Western outfit beneath the heavy brown sweater. Why would she trek through the middle of nowhere wearing a knee-length denim skirt and cowgirl boots? None of this made any sense.

Janel wasn't the type of person murderers chased down to kill. She must have been in the wrong place at the wrong time. Zach placed his hand over hers. Was she safe now? Or were her troubles just beginning?

TWO

By late afternoon, the stabbing pain in Janel's head finally lessened to a relentless ache. Sitting back in a cushioned reclining chair, she stared up at the blue curtains that separated her from the other patients in the emergency department. The doctor had urged her to rest, but she couldn't. She feared if she fell asleep, her returning memories would slip away again. It was bad enough she still couldn't recall the past two days. She almost died and didn't know why.

"You'll feel better before long." The calming voice belonged to Zach.

He'd been standing vigil close by since she'd arrived by ambulance, even waiting there while she underwent tests. The doctor would be back soon to go over the results.

She glanced over at Zach, and another memory flickered through her mind. They were working at a church festival they cochaired. He handed her a plate of cookies for the bake sale and joked about how they were safe to eat because his sister donated them, not him. "We made a lot of money that day," she murmured.

Zach tilted his head. "What?"

"The fall festival. We brought in a lot of money for the food bank."

He eased into a smile. "We did. When you're all better, we can plan the next one."

She agreed and settled back in the chair. Zach made her feel safe, and not just because he stood six foot three, had broad shoulders and a commanding presence in his official uniform. He was a solid connection to her normal life. Their conversations at church were always easygoing, nothing too personal, and she enjoyed his company. He made her laugh—during less serious times. And now he'd put his life on the line for her.

Zach lowered his large frame into the cushioned chair beside her. He was ruggedly handsome with his thick dark hair and square jaw. "Have you remembered what happened this morning?"

"I'm afraid not. I can't get over the fact a murderer shot and killed a landscape worker and then tried to kill me." She bit her lip, thinking about what Zach had told her when she questioned him earlier. "I'm so grateful you were there. You saved my life."

"I was doing my job," he responded in his usual humble manner, then added, "I'm glad I was there, too."

She nervously brushed her fingers over the

denim skirt covering her legs. "I wish I knew why I was in the forest. It's not like I'm dressed for a hike. Not that I have the interest or time to go on one."

"Could you have made plans to meet your boyfriend at one of the camping sites? I tried to reach him at the university, but no one answered the phone in his department."

The mere mention of the man she'd wasted over five years dating made her headache worse. That was a memory she would have liked to keep hidden in the back of her mind. "We broke up last month."

"I'm sorry," he said, his tone sympathetic.

"It's for the best. I need to focus my energy on the gallery, instead of the drama that comes with dating and breaking up." Because she didn't trust her instincts, she feared she might attract another man like Todd.

She should have realized earlier that their relationship was doomed. He worked tirelessly, ensuring he remained on the tenure track, while she kept busy trying to attract new customers to her gallery, Red Rock Artistry. He lived in Flagstaff, and she lived farther down the mountain in Sedona. But they never argued, and she trusted him, so she was blindsided when he fell in love with a former student. Obviously, he wasn't spending all his free time writing articles for academic journals.

The curtain opened and Janel's fraternal twin sister peered in at them.

"Karla! You're here." Relief washed over her.

It had only been a week since they last saw each other, but right now, it seemed like an eternity.

Zach stood, surprise flickering across his face. His gaze shifted from one sister to the other.

Janel was used to this reaction. They both strongly resembled their mother. Strangers often mistook them for identical twins until they stood side by side, and then their slight differences became apparent. Karla was two inches taller and had hazel-colored eyes. Janel's were blue.

"Your assistant manager called me from the gallery." Karla rushed over in the signature black turtleneck sweater and black jeans she wore with her blond hair, the same color as Janel's, tied up in a ponytail. "Are you all right?"

"I'm fine." She was too embarrassed to admit she lost a fight with a tree and hit her forehead.

"Deputy, are you guarding my sister?" Karla's tone was gruff. She was older by ten minutes, but it might as well have been a decade. She had been looking out for Janel since they were toddlers.

Zach held his hat in his hands and answered, "There's no reason to believe she's in any danger here, ma'am."

"Karla, this is Zach Walker. He's the deputy sheriff who saved me. He's also my friend from church. I told you about him."

"I'm sorry I sounded harsh." Regret flickered across her face. "My sister's safety is my top priority."

"Completely understandable." His gaze traveled between the sisters again. "I'm surprised we haven't met before."

Janel didn't want to bring up the touchy topic of her sister not attending church or the fact she thought Sedona was too small. "She lives down in the valley, in Scottsdale. We usually get together there."

"We can talk about that later." Karla examined the bump on Janel's forehead, then turned to Zach. "Who did this to her? Have you caught them?"

"Not at this time." Zach's tone remained professional. "But we know he's headed north, and the Fugitive Retrieval Team is hot on his trail."

The doctor stepped through the opening in the curtain and joined the group. Janel was relieved to see the man with the answers. Based on the touch of gray at his temples, she had guessed him to be in his early fifties. She'd instantly liked him when he first examined her; he spoke in a soothing voice while avoiding the use of scary-sounding medical jargon.

"Miss Newman, how are you feeling? Any changes since we last spoke?"

"My head feels like someone's tapping on it with their knuckles instead of a hammer, like it did an hour ago. I guess that's progress."

The doctor glanced at Karla and did a double take.

"This is my sister," Janel explained. "You can

speak freely. We're all eager to hear the test results."

With a nod, he began, "I confirmed you have a concussion. Your headache, any dizziness and most, if not all, of your memory loss should be temporary, but you must relax and let your brain heal."

Karla studied her when the doctor mentioned memory loss.

"Should," Janel repeated. "Are you saying I may never remember what happened today?"

"That's a possibility, but nothing to worry about. It's not uncommon for patients to forget the event that caused the injury."

"Is it normal to forget two days?" Janel hoped it wasn't a symptom of a more severe condition, while she tried to ignore the growing look of concern on her sister's face.

The doctor gestured toward Zach. "The deputy sheriff said you were running from a gunman. Your memory loss is understandable when you consider your brain is trying to recover from both a concussion and an extremely traumatic situation. Keep in mind when you first regained consciousness, you couldn't remember who you were."

"How long will it take for the rest of her memories to return—if they do?" Karla asked.

"Each case is different, but it's been my experience that she might remember more over the next few days." He turned back to Janel. "Unless your subconscious doesn't want you to, or if you try to get back to a normal routine too quickly. Also, there may be moments when you have trouble focusing or you feel confused as your memories return. That's normal and won't affect your brain's ability to function and store new memories."

"That's a relief. When can I go home?"

"Soon, unless your symptoms worsen. Do you have any other questions?"

Janel shook her head, then looked to her sister, who said, "Not right now."

"When you get home, you'll want to schedule a follow-up appointment with your regular doctor." He stepped toward the curtain. "I'll be back shortly with your discharge papers."

Janel thanked him before he left. She still couldn't wrap her head around the fact she'd lost two whole days. "I don't know how I'll relax if I can't stop wondering why I was in the forest. It's driving me crazy."

Karla planted a hand on her hip. "Something unexpected must have taken you there. When I spoke to Charlene, she said you had left work to go to the bank and planned to come straight back."

The mention of her assistant manager's name had Janel thinking about her gallery and the trouble they were facing. But then her throbbing headache reminded her of the doctor's recommendation to relax.

Attempting to do so, she watched her sister and Zach discuss the businesses closest to that part of the woods.

Keeping his word, the doctor returned about fifteen minutes later. After he cleared her to leave, Karla announced she would drive Janel home.

Zach offered to walk them to the parking lot, which made Janel feel safer. "Sheriff's deputies will step up patrols in your neighborhood, just in case, and if anything out of the ordinary happens, call me right away."

Karla took the business card he offered. "We will. I'm taking the rest of the week off to stay with her."

"You don't need to do that," Janel protested, not wanting to be a burden.

"I want to. You're family. Not to mention you would do the same for me." Karla collected the paperwork from her and then they all stepped into the hall. Because Janel wasn't admitted to the hospital, there was no need for a wheelchair.

Outside the emergency department's automatic doors, the cold winter weather enveloped Janel while the hum of Flagstaff's rush hour traffic reminded her of the late hour. It would take longer to reach her house near Sedona. At least forty-five minutes, maybe an hour.

Zach scanned the lot, filled with cars. "Where did you park?"

"The back corner. Stay here, and I'll get the car." Karla took a step and Janel touched her arm to stop her.

"I want to go home. It'll be faster if I walk with you." Facing two troubled expressions, Janel tried to assure them that she'd be fine. "I haven't run into a single tree since we left the building."

Karla relented. Zach smiled at her remark, but he stuck close to her side as they passed by a parked ambulance in the circular drive.

Her sister guided them toward the first row of vehicles. Before advancing between a truck and a delivery van, she held up her key fob. "My car's been sitting awhile in the cold. I'll start the heater."

Karla pointed it toward the far end of the lot and pressed the button.

The ground quaked as a hot blast shot through the air, sending metal flying, and knocking Janel off her feet with a powerful force.

Instinctively, Zach caught Janel in his arms before she hit the asphalt. A fiery cloud blanketed the sky as he whisked her away between the oversize vehicles parked in the front row. Karla regained her balance and rushed after them.

"Stay low and out of sight," he instructed as he shifted into a crouched position to keep from being seen by whoever planted the bomb in Karla's car. He placed his hand on Janel's shoulder and looked her in the eyes. "Are you hurt? Did anything hit you?"

"No," she murmured. Clearly stunned, she sat on the cold, hard ground, hidden between the truck and delivery van. "Did someone just try to kill us?"

"It looks that way." He coughed on the acrid smoke wafting through the air, then turned to Karla, who sat next to her sister. "How about you? Are you all right?"

She removed a cell phone from her pocket. "Shaken, but okay. I can't believe someone blew up my car! I'm calling 911."

"Tell the dispatcher you're with me and ask to be connected to Lieutenant Yeager with the sheriff's office." Zach removed his Glock from his holster, then left Janel in the care of her sister to peer around the truck for anyone who looked like they didn't belong.

A young couple rushed from their car to the safety of the group gathering outside of the emergency department's doors. Security guards spoke in their communication devices while spreading out through the lot. EMTs scanned the area for potential victims of the blast. Zach hadn't seen any.

Movement in the bushes that separated the hospital from the administrative offices caught his attention. He shifted to get a better view and spotted a man of average height and build in a black hoodie and distinctive oversize sunglasses with mirror-blue lenses. Somehow, the fugitive had escaped the sheriff's deputies, who were still heading north.

Zach yelled toward the crowd, "Get back inside! Now!"

A shot rang out, and he dropped low behind the truck. A bullet whizzed over his shoulder and hit the van behind him. The side mirror landed on the asphalt with a noisy clatter.

Screams erupted from the stragglers still outside the emergency department's entrance, and this time, the guards yelled for them to hurry back inside.

"Zach!" Janel's voice rose in panic.

He turned and leaned toward her. "I'm okay."

"What are we going to do? This guy is going to kill us." Fear had Janel's hands shaking. The shooter must think she can identify him, or he wouldn't have risked coming to the hospital.

"Have faith. I'll get us out of this alive." Zach's words reminded him to pray for guidance. The danger they faced was escalating, and they needed help.

Karla handed him her phone. "It's the lieutenant."

Wasting no time, he grabbed the device and rattled off, "We're being shot at. It's our fugitive. Same black hoodie and sunglasses." Sirens in the distance announced help was coming, but would they arrive in time? "I need to get Janel Newman and her twin out of here. He just blew up the sister's car."

"The sheriff's office has a lobby full of reporters waiting for a press conference," his friend and supervisor stated, his voice pitched higher than normal. "I'll need time to find a safe location to hide them."

Zach's family had experience with this type of situation. His brothers had both hid women in danger at the ranch. The shoot-outs and bombing that followed led to the family equine business losing longtime customers. They were struggling financially, and it was up to him to find the solution to turn things around since his father had retired and left him in charge. Any additional trouble, resulting in further loss of revenue, would ruin them.

Feeling the weight of this decision on his shoulders, he chose to put their futures in God's hands. "I can take the sisters to the ranch."

"I was hoping you'd say that." Lieutenant Yeager sounded relieved. "I'll call your brother Cole to warn him you're coming in hot before I update the sheriff. We'll do what we can to help."

After disconnecting the call, Zach handed the phone back to Karla. "We're leaving. I need you both to do exactly as I say and try not to make a sound."

He peered through the truck window, looking for their shooter, who was no longer standing in the same spot. Then, after assuring himself that his SUV was where he'd left it, Zach motioned for the sisters to follow. "Stay low."

Janel pushed to her feet and hunched between him and Karla. They wove like a snake between and behind vehicles. Another shot fired.

The bullet pinged off a streetlamp three feet away.

Zach jerked back, then thrust out his arm to halt their progression.

The wail of sirens grew louder. Help was much closer. But the fugitive could still shoot and kill them at any moment—even once the deputies arrived. After a minute elapsed without gunfire, Zach continued forward, rounding the bumper of a compact car. He glanced back toward the bushes but didn't see any movement.

"Let's go!" They hustled while hiding as much as possible behind one car, then another until they reached his SUV. He could hear Janel's footfalls behind him.

He stopped the sisters once again, this time to look under the car's carriage. His key fob wouldn't turn on the engine, or he would have done so earlier to check for a bomb. Not seeing anything, he opened the driver's side door and searched the inside.

Confident the SUV was safe, he ushered them into the back seat. "Stay out of sight."

After closing their door, Zach climbed behind the wheel and turned over the engine. Shifting into Reverse, he realized he had held his breath while turning the key. Breathing normally again, he backed out, shifted into Drive and then sped out of the lot onto the busy road, just as a parade of sheriff's vehicles stormed the parking lot through the other entrance.

He checked the rearview mirror and caught sight of a white sedan careening out of the hospital's administrative parking lot. The same area where the fugitive had recently hidden behind the bushes. The sun reflected off the driver's mirrored sunglasses. "Hang on! He's following us."

Hearing Janel and her sister buckling up in the back seat, he pressed on the gas, swerved around one car, then another, until he reached the intersection. With a green turn arrow displayed on the traffic light, he pulled the steering wheel into a sharp U-turn. The fastest way to his family ranch outside of Sedona would be the interstate, not the switchbacks down the mountain.

They raced out of town, increasing the gap between his SUV and the sedan that had missed the U-turn. Zach kept the engine roaring while his gaze constantly checked the rearview mirror. He couldn't count on maintaining their lead on the long stretch of interstate.

With a sign for Kachina Village looming ahead, a plan developed. He swerved onto the exit and drove into the quiet neighborhood. After several turns, he found what he was looking for: a cabin with no cars parked out front and a boat stored on the side. He maneuvered the SUV into position and backed up beside the boat, which would allow for a quick exit.

"What are you doing?" Janel asked.

"Hiding until the coast is clear." Zach reached for the folded sun shade he had left on the passenger seat, then flipped it open. After securing it in the front window, he called the lieutenant and filled him in on the white sedan. "It has an orange flower decal on the front bumper."

"We had a report of a stolen vehicle matching that description. Stay put until you hear from me."

Zach disconnected the call and turned in his seat to check on his passengers. Janel had a deer-in-headlights expression. "We shouldn't be here too long."

She nodded, not looking convinced.

Karla squeezed her sister's hand. "No one can say you're boring."

A smile tugged at Janel's lips. "Not funny."

"Kind of," her sister replied with a shrug.

Janel's eyes suddenly grew wide as she pointed to the passenger window.

THREE

Stunned into silence, Janel, sitting in the back seat, could only point toward the tinted passenger side window. The white sedan rolling down the residential street was about to pass by in front of them. They hadn't seen it sooner because they had parked beside a boat on a trailer, which blocked their view. The murderer was only ten feet away.

"Down!" Zach ordered in a low voice from the front seat, clearly concerned that the SUV's darkly tinted windows and sunshade fully covering the front window might not be enough to hide them.

Janel unbuckled her seat belt and slid down onto the floorboard. Her sister followed her lead, the stress of the moment showing on her face.

From her position behind the passenger seat, Janel watched Zach. He sat perfectly still, watching and waiting.

Loose gravel on the residential road crunched below the wheels of the sedan as it slowly drove past them. Janel feared the shooter would recognize their vehicle and shoot Zach, then her, then Karla.

If they lived, she'd thank Zach for backing in when he parked. Their position hid the license plate. The shooter surely must have seen it during the chase in Flagstaff.

She strained to hear every sound. The rattle of the sedan's engine slowly faded. The murderer had turned a corner and was now driving down the side road.

With each second, he drifted farther away. You'd think her heart would stop thundering and her breathing would return to normal, but no. She felt lightheaded, the way she had in the emergency room.

She reached up to touch the goose egg on her forehead. *Relax.* The doctor's instructions echoed in her mind. This couldn't be what he had envisioned. A silent chuckle racked her body, and she feared she was losing her mind. Tears slid down her cheeks.

"He's gone," Karla murmured. "Everything's okay now."

"Is it?" Janel glanced at her sister. "For how long?"

Sirens coming from the nearby interstate gave her hope. After a couple of long, frightening minutes, Zach turned to speak to them while holding up his phone. "The lieutenant just texted. A deputy reported seeing a white sedan speeding away from this location."

"What now?" Janel focused on his familiar warm brown eyes, which further eased her fears.

"I contacted my brother Jackson. He runs a Northern Arizona task force. His group volunteered to watch the roads between here and the ranch to make sure we're not followed. We'll sit here until they're all in place."

"It's good to have connections." Karla climbed off the floor.

Janel rose and peered out the windows, double-checking to make sure it was safe to leave her hiding spot. Her legs cramped as she stretched them. "Zach, are you sure you want to take us to the ranch? There's a murderer after me. We'll be putting your family in danger."

"My family has had plenty of experience fighting bad guys." Zach sent her a gentle smile, which she returned as she eased into her seat. She'd heard stories about the shoot-outs at his ranch and hoped that kind of trouble wouldn't follow them there.

Silence settled over the SUV as incoming storm clouds altered the golden hue of the sunset to create a powerful image in the sky. With time ticking by at an agonizingly slow pace, it soon became apparent that the murderer wasn't returning. With nothing to do but wait, Janel's thoughts bounced between past and present, although the past two days still eluded her.

Janel had to admit she felt better knowing Jackson's team would look out for them when they drove to the ranch. She'd met Zach's brother at church. He'd married a woman he had protected while working for the DEA. From all accounts, they were a happy couple with a long lifetime together to look forward to.

Once upon a time, Janel thought she'd be living a fairy tale with Todd, but it all went wrong. His cheating proved he wasn't the man she thought he was. Did she miss the signs from day one? Did he say what she wanted to hear, so she'd be available until he found someone better? Why didn't she see through him?

Todd wasn't her only misstep. She and Karla had grown up surrounded by Western art. Their mother became a famous Sedona-based artist after her divorce, and their father was a museum curator in Scottsdale. Eight years ago, Janel opened her gallery, a place where she could display her mother's paintings, along with the works of other Southwestern artists.

No one expected a larger gallery to open down the street. When sales dropped, Janel convinced herself that this was a temporary condition. The newness of her competitor, Sedona Imagined, would soon wear off. Only it didn't. Before long, she was forced to reduce the number of hours for Charlene, her assistant manager.

Janel had been excited when she came up with a plan to boost sales. It included building an addition to the gallery: a room where she could hold painting classes. Her father's new wife wouldn't allow him to lend her the money, and Karla didn't have any to spare. So, she turned to the bank. The biggest mistake of her life. If only she could forget *that* again.

"Buckle your seat belts." Zach's remark jerked her out of her thoughts and reminded her they had to venture out into the open, away from the shadow of the boat stored beside them.

She did as he said and drew in a deep, settling breath. He turned over the engine and headed down the street. They passed several cars, most likely driven by people who lived in the cabin community. No one gave them a second look. He knew what he was doing, hiding here.

When they reached the interstate, her pulse picked up along with the speed of the SUV. She kept an eye out for the white sedan, despite knowing Jackson's team was making sure they weren't followed. Karla looked out the back window while Zach focused on the road ahead. No one spoke as lightning lit up the night sky miles away.

Janel took her cues from Zach. As long as he acted like they were out of danger, she could believe they were. For now.

Forty minutes later, Zach drove under a wooden arch: the gateway to Walker Ranch. A porch illuminated up ahead called to them like a beacon.

With darkness blanketing the pasture, the horses were nowhere to be seen. She spotted a barn beyond the white wooden fence and pictured them resting for the night. As they neared the house, a garage door lifted with the familiar sound of grinding gears.

Zach drove inside, rolling closer to Mr. Walker, who stood beside an open door, waiting for them. The older, distinguished-looking cowboy pushed the button to close the garage once the SUV was safely parked.

Janel exhaled, louder than she'd intended. She felt like an intolerable weight had been lifted off her shoulders.

Karla grinned. "We made it."

"Thanks to Zach and his brother." She would be forever grateful.

"Let's get you both inside." Zach pushed open his door. "You must be hungry. I know I am."

She wasn't ready for food, but she was more than ready to leave the SUV. She climbed out and headed toward Mr. Walker, who gently touched her shoulder.

"Thank you so much for taking us in." Janel's voice hinted at the exhaustion she felt. She could only imagine how tired her eyes looked.

"It's no problem at all, little lady." He offered his hand to Karla. "Welcome to our home."

"You have quite the family. I can honestly say we are alive thanks to your son here." Karla gestured toward Zach, and his father sent him a proud nod.

Mrs. Walker waved them into the kitchen. "You're here!" She pulled Janel into a hug like her mother would have if she were still with them. "We were so worried about you. Cole told us all about your sister's car exploding. How terrifying."

"Terrifying sums it up." Overcome with emotion, Janel felt a tear slide down her cheek. Mrs. Walker had always been kind to her. She'd even brought meals over to the house when she'd heard that the twins were losing their mother to cancer. That was three years ago, and Karla had been around more during that horrible time. "Mrs. Walker, you've met my sister before."

Janel stepped aside as Zach's mother took Karla's hand between hers. "Of course, I remember."

This family was beyond kind.

Fear twisted in Janel's gut. "Mrs. Walker, I think we should leave. I don't want to put your family in danger by being here."

Zach's mother wiped a tear from Janel's cheek. "Nonsense. God made all three of my sons law enforcement officers, and everyone in this family can shoot a gun and hit their target. Now, let's get you two settled in so you can rest. Dinner will be ready soon."

She escorted the twins through the kitchen, which smelled of warm rolls baking in the oven, and into the spacious living room.

Karla collapsed onto a comfortable brown leather sofa. "Janel, how did this happen?"

"I wish I could tell you. I just don't know." Janel sat beside her, the hopelessness of the situation ripping her apart. She spotted Zach watching them from the dining room and asked, "How and why did he blow up my sister's car?"

"Well, we know he stole the white sedan after leaving the forest." Zach sat on the edge of a wing-back chair. "My best guess is he heard the news reports on the radio about you being taken to the hospital. Once he was there, he spotted Karla arriving and knew she had to be there to see you. You two look a lot alike."

"Where did he get the bomb?" Janel asked. "I doubt he found it inside the trunk of the car he stole."

"I suspect he had easy access to one and picked it up on the way."

Fear and confusion had Janel's headache pounding again. "But how did he know she would drive me home?"

"He wouldn't have known for sure." Zach rubbed the pad of his thumb over his chin. "If you saw his face and can identify him, blowing up Karla's car would serve as a warning—if you didn't die in the explosion."

If she could tell the murderer she couldn't identify him, would he believe her? Would he go away and leave her alone? Probably not.

After breakfast the next morning, Zach sat at the kitchen table across from Janel and Karla, who had changed into jeans and long-sleeved shirts his mother had rounded up for them. He gulped his third cup of coffee, needing every drop. His father and sister, Lily, had volunteered to divide up the night into shifts where they watched their recently installed security monitor. But between the rain pelting the ranch all night and jerking awake at every unusual sound, he still didn't get much sleep.

His brother Cole stepped into the room, and Zach introduced him to Karla, adding that he was Sedona's lead detective.

"Is this a personal visit or professional?" Karla asked.

"Both." Cole poured himself a cup of coffee and leaned against the counter. "Janel, how are you feeling this morning?"

"Tired." She touched the goose egg left behind after she collided with the tree. The swelling had gone down, but not completely. "My head doesn't hurt nearly as much as it did yesterday, though.

The over-the-counter pain relievers your mother gave me are helping."

"That's good. And your memory?" Cole watched her closely. "I heard you lost two days."

"I'm certain I took cinnamon rolls to the gallery yesterday or the day before. I'm hoping that means I'll remember more soon."

A wary expression flickered across her face. Zach could understand if she feared those returning memories. A murderer was trying to kill her, and no one knew why.

Cole's gaze shifted to Zach. "Have you discussed the gallery?"

"Not yet, but I agree with you. The two events must be related." Zach never believed in coincidences. He opened his phone, which contained the app that would allow him to view the security monitor. His deep-seated fear was drawing a murderer to the ranch. Both Janel and their equine business depended on a safe environment.

"What two events are you talking about?" Janel asked, making it apparent she hadn't remembered the burglary yet.

Karla tapped a fingernail on the table before reluctantly answering her sister. "Janel, your gallery was broken into early Monday morning. Four VanZandt bronze statues and Mom's paintings were stolen."

Her jaw dropped. "Mom's... No. That was her legacy."

"I drove here immediately after you called yesterday morning. That was hours before you ended up in the forest and lost your memory." Karla's gaze shifted between Cole and Zach. "In my job as an insurance investigator, I've been looking into a recent string of burglaries. At least one art thief, maybe more, has been hitting galleries and private collectors in New Mexico, Arizona, Colorado and Utah. The most valuable items were taken each time and only enough to fit in the trunk of a car. Janel is my sister, so I won't be working her case."

Zach had seen how brave Janel was after her mother's cancer diagnosis. She took on the role of caretaker while working remotely. Then came the depressing months following the funeral. But she picked herself up and focused on her business. Now this. He wanted to fix everything for her. The truth was, he wanted to go out with her, but he couldn't enter another rebound relationship. He refused to risk his heart like that ever again.

Visibly upset, Janel reached up and touched the bump on her head.

"Is the gallery burglary similar to the others?" Zach knew about the break-in; his brother had mentioned it the other night when he began his investigation. What Karla was sharing was new information.

"I don't know yet," Karla admitted. "The guy I'm looking for wears black from head to toe, including a ski mask, and circumvents the alarm system by cutting wires and jamming the backup signal. A security guard in Santa Fe changed his routine one night and walked in on him. He was overpowered and tied up."

"There are two big differences between those burglaries and this one." Cole had their full, undivided attention. "If Zach's fugitive is the gallery's burglar, he shot and killed someone. And, according to the security company, Janel's code was used to disarm the alarm. Only the cameras were jammed or turned off."

"That's not possible. No one knows my code but me and my assistant manager." Janel glared at the brothers after they exchanged knowing looks. "Charlene would *never* steal from me."

"Janel…" Zach kept his voice calm, projecting both his role as a lawman and as her friend. "Cole has a job to do. It would help if you told him all about Charlene and why you trust her."

"Okay." After composing herself, she began. "Charlene is so competent, she's the only person I've had to hire. She has an art degree and one day, when she has enough money for a down payment, she'll open her own gallery. There isn't anything she doesn't know about the business."

Janel must have realized she'd just provided Cole with a motive for Charlene to steal, because she rushed to add, "I've known no one who is more trustworthy or more reliable. Charlene handles large money transactions, private information and valuable merchandise. And I've never had an issue with her. Not once."

Zach's mind raced over the possibilities. He knew one thing for sure: if Charlene was innocent, suspicion would fall on Janel. "Could anyone else have gained access to your alarm code?"

"Todd," Karla answered for her sister. "Did you change your code after you two split?"

"No, but he wouldn't steal from me, either."

Karla sent her an I'm-not-so-sure-about-that look. "He wasn't who you thought he was, and I saw you enter your code without hiding it from him."

Janel held her head in her hands before releasing a long, slow breath. "You're saying the burglary, the murderer chasing me in the forest and the car bomb are most likely connected. Todd called me two weeks ago, trying to get back together. A man who claims to have feelings for you doesn't steal your mother's paintings and then try to kill you."

Her ex called her? Zach felt an ache in the pit of his stomach as his own past reared its ugly head. A few years before he met Janel, he dated a woman who had recently broken up with her boyfriend. Everything went well for six joyful months. He was beginning to think they had a future together when she dumped him to go back to her ex. She'd failed to mention that this other man had been calling her, promising to be faithful.

Zach had learned a valuable lesson: don't date anyone coming out of a long relationship, especially not a woman still communicating with her ex when he's trying to win her back.

He forced his mind off the past and pictured Janel's gallery. He'd been there several times. "How long have you had your security system?"

"About ten months. Our father paid to have the system upgraded after Karla told us about the string of burglaries."

"Did you select your code or use one the security company gave you?" Zach asked.

"I chose it, but the technician who installed the system walked me through the steps."

Karla leaned closer. "Did he watch you enter it, or did he step away?"

"I don't know." Janel pressed fingers against her temple. Her headache must have returned. After a few seconds, she dropped her hand and locked gazes with Zach. "I paid this company to protect my inventory. One-of-a-kind art. It never dawned on me they might steal from me."

He worried this discussion might be too much for her. The stress could delay her recovery, and he cared for her too much to see that happen. "We don't know that they had anything to do with the burglary."

Cole's cell phone rang, and he left the kitchen to take the call.

While he was gone, Zach asked if her code might be easy to figure out—like her birthday.

"No. The security panel has numbers and letters, so I used our mother's childhood nickname. She never shared it with anyone but us." Janel gestured toward her sister. "And of course, I told… Charlene!" Her eyes widened. "What time is it?"

Zach checked his cell phone. "A quarter to nine. Why?"

"Charlene's on her way to work. It's not safe. That murderer figured out which car belonged to my sister. He probably knows about the gallery—especially if these events are connected. He might be waiting there for me—with a gun."

"Charlene has blond hair like we do," Karla added. "He could mistake her for Janel." She unlocked her smartphone. "What's her cell number? We might be able to reach her before she gets there."

Janel groaned. "You know I don't memorize numbers. They're in my Contacts, and I lost my phone yesterday." She turned to Zach for help. "If he kills her, it will be all my fault. We have to find her and warn her!"

Zach shook his head, stiffening both his back and his resolve. "We're staying here. I will not risk your life."

FOUR

"The police should be at the gallery by now."
Janel's foot shook with impatience while sitting
at the ranch's kitchen table. Zach had called his
lieutenant over two minutes ago. "Why didn't I
think to close the gallery after the explosion?"

"You have a concussion. Besides, you were
dealing with a lot yesterday," Zach reminded her.

"We all were," Karla added. "Now, try not to
worry. I'm sure Charlene's fine." Her tone was
reassuring, but the concern in her expression belied her words.

"I can't relax. That…murderer blew up your
car. He's determined to kill me and may have
planted more bombs." She sent a worried glance
Zach's way. "I watched a news report last night
on Karla's phone. They named my gallery."

"I understand your concern, and I've always
admired the way you care for others. It's one of
your finest qualities," Zach stated calmly. "As
for Charlene, the Sedona Police Department increased their patrols around your gallery last

night. No one reported anything out of the ordinary." His phone rang, and he checked the screen. "I'll be right back."

Just because no one saw anything when they drove by her gallery didn't mean there wasn't another bomb. Trepidation churned in her gut. "I can't take this waiting any longer." An idea occurred to her. "Can I use your phone?"

"Why?" Karla held it close. "You can't call the gallery. Charlene might rush inside to answer the phone. If there's a bomb…"

"I wouldn't endanger her like that." The mental image was too much for Janel to handle. She pressed her hand to her now throbbing forehead. "I only want to check the security camera footage. If it's even working. The burglars managed to shut it off when they broke in."

Karla handed her the phone.

After logging into the security website, Janel was relieved to see the inside of the gallery pop up on the screen. Charlene was standing at the glass door, turning the key in the lock. She tugged the door open.

Janel held her breath, her heart thundering in her chest.

Karla squeezed Janel's arm like a vise.

One. Two. Three.

Nothing happened. No explosion. No hidden madman shooting.

Afraid to relax too soon, Janel remained frozen in place.

Charlene punched the security code into the pad hanging on the wall. Meanwhile, her boyfriend, Robert, a tall, good-looking man in his late thirties, turned the Closed sign to Open.

After walking behind the counter, Charlene locked her purse away in a cabinet beneath the cash register as two Sedona police officers rushed into the gallery, glancing about for trouble. They took the assistant manager and her boyfriend totally by surprise. Soon, a sheriff's deputy joined them. Janel wished she could hear what they were saying.

Moments later, when it became obvious Charlene was safe, Janel exhaled, releasing the mountain of stress that had built up inside her. Janel reached for her sister's hand, still gripping her arm. "You can let go now."

Karla rubbed the area she had squeezed. "Did I hurt you?"

"Nah." Fingernails breaking the skin was nothing compared to the fear of possibly seeing a bomb kill someone close to her, not to mention the destruction of her livelihood.

Zach stepped back into the kitchen. "Everything's fine at the gallery."

"Thank you for sending the police and deputies." Janel held up her sister's phone. "And, as you can see, my cameras are working now. I'm not sure what that means for your brother's investigation into the burglary."

"I'll text him after I tell you some good news you don't already know." Zach's mood was lighter as he slipped back into his seat at the table. "The fugitive's white sedan was found abandoned and burned outside Las Vegas."

"Burned?" Janel lifted a brow.

"To eliminate fingerprints and DNA evidence," Karla supplied.

Zach acknowledged her statement as fact with a nod. "There was enough left of the car to confirm it was the one stolen in Flagstaff yesterday. Unfortunately, we haven't located any video showing the driver's face without the hoodie and sunglasses, so we still can't identify him."

"We could pass each other on the street one day, and I won't know it's him." The phone felt heavy in Janel's hand. This was the first time she'd logged into the security monitoring website since being told about the burglary after her memory loss. She peered into the screen again and noticed the walls where her mother's paintings once hung were now bare. A sense of loss overwhelmed her. She'd only felt that empty one other time. The moment her mother had passed away.

"I'm calling Charlene." She closed the website and located the gallery's number on the phone.

When her assistant manager answered, Janel blurted, "I was so worried about you."

"I'm not the one who was almost blown up yesterday! Are *you* safe?" Charlene's heightened sense of alarm was evident in her voice. "I tried to reach you several times, but my calls went straight to voicemail."

"I'm fine. Karla and I are staying at Walker Ranch."

Zach cringed, and Janel realized too late she probably wasn't supposed to reveal her whereabouts. Too late now. "I lost my phone. You'll need to call my sister to reach me." Janel touched the screen. "I'm placing this call on speaker. Karla and Zach, the deputy looking out for us, are in the room with me. It turns out the guy who tried to kill us is hiding in Las Vegas, but I think it would be wise to shut the gallery for a few days, just in case." It was the safest decision for everyone.

Karla shook her head at the same time Charlene rejected the idea. "We can't afford to close the doors. Besides, my boyfriend took the next week off to act as my bodyguard. And since it doesn't sound like we need one now, he can chip in and help. We've had a steady stream of customers since your story hit the news. Some are townies wishing you their best, others are tourists or reporters hoping to overhear private information. At least most are buying postcards, small prints or bookmarks."

"That's wonderful. I think." Janel winced as she touched the sore spot on her forehead. After being chased by a murderer twice, she had a hard time believing he was gone for good. The lives of every person who entered her gallery were her responsibility. "Please thank your boyfriend. I feel better knowing he can act as security if it becomes necessary." Robert had served in the military and carried a concealed weapons permit for his gun. He was levelheaded and polite.

"I'll go to the gallery to help," Karla offered. "I just need a ride."

"That can be arranged." After checking to see if anyone else wanted a refill, Zach topped off his mug.

Janel told Charlene, "Karla will head to the gallery to help you. I have to go now, but stay safe. If anything happens, call the police."

After she disconnected, Zach said, "Cole wants directions to Todd's cousin's RV. According to Todd's neighbor, he's spending a few days there."

"I can't tell him where to find the RV, but I can show him."

"Out of the question." Still holding his coffee mug, Zach stepped to the table and towered over them. "We don't know if your ex hired the murderer to break into your gallery."

Janel rolled her eyes. "I sincerely doubt he knows anyone dangerous."

"You can't be sure of that," Karla countered.

"Maybe his new girlfriend has connections to the underbelly of society."

Janel stifled a chuckle. "Do you hear yourself?"

"It's not funny when it could be true," Karla shot back.

"You're talking about Todd. Besides, they broke up. He told me so when he called."

"He claims they broke up. Don't forget, he lied and cheated. Now, let's address the matter at hand." Karla gestured to Zach. "Can you give him directions on how to get to this RV?"

"I don't think turn left at the burger joint and right at the wooden bear statue is going to help, and that's all I've got." She shrugged, knowing it wasn't what anyone wanted to hear. "The RV park is on private property, and I don't remember his cousin's name. Zach, it would be best if you drove me, and Cole followed. I could point to the RV. Todd doesn't own a gun, and the murderer is probably still in Vegas."

"We can't count on that, but as long as we don't stop and get out of the car, your idea works for me. You'll have the both of us protecting you." Zach reached for his phone. "I'll call Cole."

Ten minutes later, Zach's sister, Lily, was driving Karla to the gallery while Janel stepped into the ranch house's open garage. The feeling that she should duck hadn't left her yet. How long would it take for her to feel normal again? With the murderer's identity still hidden, would she always be afraid of strange men walking up to her?

A dark cloud hovered over her both figuratively and literally, with another storm approaching. Janel climbed into the passenger seat of Zach's SUV and pulled her long sweater over her jean-clad knees. He had offered her a coat to wear, but they were only going for a drive in a heated vehicle. No need for anything bulky.

When they approached the gate, several quarter horses stood next to the white picket fence as if greeting them. She waved, and a smile tugged at Zach's lips. If he wanted to think she was silly, that was okay with her.

She settled into her seat, preparing for the long drive. After twenty minutes of meaningless small talk, Janel finally shared, "I still don't remember the gallery burglary, but when I was on the security website this morning and saw my mother's paintings were missing from the walls, I almost broke down crying."

"No one would blame you if you did." His understanding sliced off a sliver of her emotional pain, but there was still so much left behind.

She had been worried about losing the paintings to the bank and was fighting to make sure it wouldn't happen. Now they were gone—stolen.

"I've lost so much. My mother, her paintings and maybe next, the gallery. Time and time again

I've prayed, but nothing I try helps. I feel like God has abandoned me."

Zach took his eyes off the road long enough to look her way. "God hasn't abandoned you. New, wonderful beginnings can spring from terrible circumstances. I've witnessed it many times. I promise, He has a plan for you."

"I hope you're right." Janel admired the confidence Zach exuded. Confidence she never had. "Is becoming a deputy sheriff your new beginning? The last I heard, you were in charge of your family's ranch and heading search and rescue missions."

"If you remember, we had a shoot-out and bombing at the ranch. The sheriff took notice of how I helped in those situations." Zach's smile warmed her heart. "That, along with finding a lost hiker last spring, led to a call from the sheriff. He asked if I would be interested in becoming a member of the Mounted Fugitive Retrieval Team on either a full or volunteer basis—my choice."

"I remember hearing Cole and Sierra had dated, broke up, then reunited when he saved her from a crazed bomber." She studied the sharp lines on Zach's handsome face. They'd been friends for so long, she hadn't considered how easy it would have been to fall for him if she hadn't been dating Todd. And now that she wasn't dating her ex, she didn't trust her instincts. Was Zach as good a man as she thought, or was he only showing the best side of his personality at church functions?

Her mind returned to the danger she'd faced the day before. "I'm glad you took the sheriff up on his offer. I can't imagine going through this with a total stranger."

"I admit I would have tried to trade places with anyone else assigned to protect you." After a brief pause, he added, "Breaking in a new cochair for the fall festival would be difficult work." His chuckle became contagious.

Soon she was laughing. "You can't just take a compliment, can you?"

"I guess not." He gestured toward the road. "Am I turning anywhere soon?"

"Take the next right onto the dirt road. The street sign has been missing for years."

"How many times have you been out here?"

"Three or four, for day trips. Todd likes to fish. I don't, so I would read a book in an Adirondack chair while he went out on the pond in a boat." Another example of how she and Todd had nothing in common. Why hadn't she recognized how incompatible they were? She snuck a peek at Zach and felt an emotional tug. Would she always question her judgment where men were concerned?

He steered around a corner. "Now where?"

"Continue down this road." The pine trees reminded her of the fear she'd felt the day before in another part of the forest, many miles away.

They headed closer to the hills, and she hoped she wouldn't see Todd. Ever. With the Lord's help, she would forgive him one day, but it would take time.

Minutes later, they curved their way around to a panoramic view of storm clouds heading toward the large pond the locals referred to as a lake. Recent rains and melted snow had filled in the water lost during their long, hot summer.

"I can see how hard it would be to find this place if you didn't know about it, especially with a missing street sign." Zach checked his rearview mirror.

Janel glanced at her side-view mirror and only saw Cole following them. "After you enter the park, drive toward the pond, but go slow enough for me to hunt for the armadillo."

"An armadillo?"

"Not a real one." She rolled her eyes, and he chuckled again. But the gravity of the situation soon returned. She was here to point the way for Cole. He was going to ask her ex questions that would make it obvious that he was a suspect in her burglary. Would he be angry with her? Should she care? What if he was involved?

She had been so busy defending Todd she never took the time to consider the possibility that he was involved in her burglary. A mutual friend had told Janel that he was late with his last mortgage payment after dating a woman who was high maintenance. Was he feeling the crunch financially? There were so many things about him, both past and present, that she didn't know.

"You all right?"

Zach's voice caught her attention.

"There!" She pointed to the ceramic armadillo sitting out front of a blue RV. "Turn right, then drive slowly down the road."

Cole called and Zach answered, "I'm handing you to Janel."

She nervously gripped the cell phone in her hand while she scanned the area for Todd. "We're almost there." The SUV rolled closer and closer. "It's the one with the burgundy trim on the left."

"Thanks," Cole said. "Now, you two get out of here before your ex sees you."

Zach navigated back to the road they came in on, and Janel tried to relax, but something didn't feel right. After rounding the first hill, she heard a loud pop and jerked around in her seat.

A huge spiderweb of cracked glass stretched out from a bullet hole.

Feeling her eyes grow wide, she yelled, "Someone shot at us!"

"Get down!" Zach pressed on the gas. Several glances in the rearview mirror confirmed his suspicion. They had a second assailant. This one on a hill, shooting his high-powered rifle from a kneeling position like a hunter. He was much larger than the fugitive they had encountered yesterday. Instead of a black hoodie, he wore aviator sunglasses and a camouflage jacket.

"But he was just in Las Vegas! He came back already?" Janel had slipped down in the passenger seat but kept stretching to see her side-view mirror.

"He has an accomplice." Before speeding into the next curve in the road, Zach caught sight of the shooter, pulling a helmet over light brown hair, then pushing his ride out from behind a bush and climbing on. "This one's driving a motorcycle down the hill."

"Oh, great!" Janel cried out. "How are we going to lose a shooter on two wheels?"

"We're not." His SUV had over a hundred thousand miles on the odometer. This wasn't the time to see if it could hold its own in a race. It also wasn't the time for a gunfight. Janel might get caught in the crossfire.

As they rounded the hill, he surveyed the landscape for a quick escape. Not a single side road yet, but that might work to their advantage. A side road would be too obvious.

"Over there!" Janel pointed to an area where the tree line thickened on the far side of a meadow. "Can we hide behind the trees?" The wide stretch of gravel leading up to the grass would allow them to drive off the road without leaving an obvious trail.

"Hang on!" He swerved to the right, gripping the steering wheel tightly as they bounced over uneven terrain. A *vroom* in the distance warned that the motorcycle would round the hill at any second and the driver would have a clear view of their position.

Zach's cell phone rang, and he connected it through the SUV's onboard screen with a single touch.

"I heard a gunshot," Cole yelled.

"Rifle shot! We're being chased by a shooter, wearing camouflage and driving a motorcycle. We went off-road where the forest thickens after the hills."

"I'm heading that way now."

"Call it in." Their connection ended, and Zach pressed harder on the gas while Janel gripped the center console with one hand and the SUV's grab handle with the other. He drove between two tree trunks and made a sharp left to avoid hitting an overgrown bush that had lost its leaves with the cold temperatures. They continued to weave around nature's obstacles, unable to find the perfect place to stop.

"The storm is getting closer." Janel's voice was difficult, but not impossible, to hear over the SUV's roaring engine.

Swerving around a boulder, he noticed the dark clouds. They were floating toward the nearby hills. The last thing they needed was to get stuck in a downpour.

A flash in the forest behind them, possibly sunlight reflecting off the motorcycle, sent Zach's pulse skyrocketing.

Locating a clear path to a copse of evergreens, he floored the gas pedal, climbing the mound to reach a potential hiding spot.

The SUV sped faster and faster.

At the top, he tried to circle around the bushes but couldn't.

The other side of the mound turned out to be a cliff, where floodwater rushed down a creek roughly fifteen feet below them.

Zach slammed on the brakes, but not soon enough.

They skidded over the side.

And dropped.

Janel screamed, and Zach's stomach leaped into his chest.

They landed with a jolt, and water splashed high into the air.

"You okay?" He spared a quick glance in her direction.

Wide-eyed, she nodded.

The SUV turned ninety degrees as they began to float downstream. Last night's rains had made the creek too deep to wade across.

"Water's coming in through the door!" Janel urgently lifted her boots off the floorboard.

Sirens screamed through the forest. Help was coming, but they weren't close enough.

They couldn't sit here a second longer.

"We have to get out," Zach yelled to be heard above the sound of water and debris crashing into the SUV.

She unbuckled her seat belt, then unlocked her door with a click of the power button. She pushed on the handle and then with her shoulder. "It won't open!"

"Come out on my side," he instructed and lowered his window. "There's an undertow, so stick close to me."

"Should we crawl onto the roof?" She shifted closer to the middle console, and a bullet blasted out the passenger window where she had just sat.

FIVE

"He's going to kill us!" Janel scrambled over the SUV's center console as Zach crawled out through his window. Waiting for him to clear the threshold so that she could follow sent her thumping heart into overdrive. "Hurry!"

A second bullet fired with a bang and shattered the back passenger window. Fear reverberated down her spine.

Zach reached inside, grabbed her upper arms and pulled her out into the chest-high raging waters. She gripped his broad shoulders as the frigid temperature assaulted her senses, and the undertow kept her boots from gaining purchase on the rocks below. The ping of another bullet made her shudder.

Using the SUV's door as a shield, they each took hold of the window frame to keep from being swept away. Janel leaned toward the closed back seat window, daring a quick glance at the shooter. He sat on his motorcycle up on the cliff, ready to take aim.

She panicked and ducked.

Water hit her face.

A bullet whizzed over the SUV, inches from where she'd been seconds ago.

He must have seen her.

The helmet and sunglasses he wore had kept her from getting a good look at his face. An empty rifle case hung loose over his shoulder, answering the question of how he'd managed to carry the weapon while driving his motorcycle.

Releasing her grip on the SUV with one hand, she wiped her face while kicking her feet to stay in place.

Last night's rainwater that had flooded the banks of the creek ripped apart the shrubbery and sent it sailing downstream. Zach batted away branches threatening to smack against them. Leaves clung to Janel's arm as she reached for the car again.

The SUV groaned and shifted position as it tilted with the weight of the water, filling it up like a fish tank. Her teeth chattered from the cold. They couldn't stay here long, but venturing out into the open would make them easy targets. A sense of hopelessness weighed down on her.

Zach gestured toward a sharp bend in the creek about twenty-five feet away.

She studied the area where the water turned away from the cliffs, which were a series of rock faces, some with enormous gaps between them.

The shooter couldn't follow them easily on the motorcycle if they moved downstream. He'd have to backtrack into the forest, travel in a parallel direction and then find another path to the creek. That would give them time to escape.

Zach leaned close enough for her to hear him ask, "Can you swim?"

She nodded, despite knowing the feat might be too much for her. The current was strong, but they couldn't stay here, freezing and treading water, hoping help would find them in time. The SUV was unstable. If it dropped below the waterline, they would have nothing to hide behind. "How do we get there without him killing us?"

"When I start shooting, you swim as fast as you can. After you turn the corner, find a spot where he can't see you and get out on your right side. I'll catch up with you." Zach pulled his gun from a shoulder holster.

Could he swim and fire his weapon at the same time? An image of him fatally wounded and drowning flashed through her mind. Terror struck her. "Don't die on me, Zach Walker!"

He looked her in the eyes and promised, "I won't."

Did he really believe he would live? She tried to read his face, but he turned and held his gun above the SUV's roofline.

"Wait!" The drenched sweater she wore over the shirt she'd borrowed was too heavy to swim in. She slipped it off her shoulders and pushed it inside the SUV through the open window. "Ready."

With the sound of his first shot, she jerked into action. She pushed away from the sinking vehicle with her feet and swam through the murky water, summoning every ounce of energy she could muster. More than once, she shoved floating branches away from her face and felt the sting of their scratches.

A bullet whizzed overhead, and Zach fired back two shots.

She pushed aside her trepidation and swam hard. *Don't look back.*

Knowing she was out in the open with a gunfight taking place over her shoulder, she wanted to duck but knew she'd see nothing below the surface. Instead, she kicked faster and worked her arms harder. *God, please save us.*

After she turned the corner, she let the swift flowing water carry her another thirty feet. She could no longer see the shooter on the cliff, which hopefully meant he couldn't see her, either. Her mission now was to find clear access to dry land. When the flooded shrubbery reaching up out of the water thinned, she stopped floating and fought against the current to swim ashore. More gunfire rang out in the distance.

She crawled up onto the bank, her breathing rapid and shallow. After shifting into a sitting position, she wiped the dead grass and dirt off her hands, then pushed wet hair away from her eyes and listened. The seconds between shots lengthened. Her fear for Zach was overwhelming.

Janel could hear multiple police cruisers now but couldn't see them.

With the roar of the raging waters and high-pitched sirens filling her ears, she barely detected the motorcycle's engine as it came alive and took off. Surveying the scenery, she spied Zach swimming down the creek, less than twenty feet away. *He's alive.*

"Over here!" Janel jumped to her feet and waved both arms until he spotted her. When he was close, she grabbed his soaking wet coat and tried to help him up out of the water. It soon became clear he had the situation under control, so she stood back and watched this tower of strength rise out of the creek. He was here, with her, and they were safe.

Dripping wet, he took her hand. "We need to find cover in case he comes back."

With those words, her brief solace disappeared. They weren't out of danger like she'd thought.

They rushed toward an enormous tree and hid behind its wide trunk. Freezing from head to toe, Janel slumped to the ground and curled up in a ball, wishing she were invisible.

Zach remained standing, scanning their surroundings. Seconds later, the sirens traveled in a new direction. "Looks like the deputies spotted him."

"I hope so." Her aching legs cramped. She stretched them out, but when the wind swept over her wet clothing, she shuddered and curled up again. The tree's rough bark scratched her back. "Do you think he's gone for good?"

"Maybe for the moment, but we still need to be on high alert."

If these men weren't arrested soon, she'd always wonder when they would show up to finish the job. Would they ring her doorbell at home first? Walk into the gallery with a gun? Approach her on the street with a knife? "You said this shooter wasn't the fugitive you were chasing near Flagstaff. The one who tried to kill me and blew up Karla's car."

"That's right. This guy is much bigger." Lines furrowed in Zach's forehead as he looked down at her from where he stood, leaning against the tree and keeping an eye out for the shooter.

"Do you think your fugitive, the murderer, came back from Vegas? Assuming he's the one who burned the stolen car there. Could he be here, too?" Her teeth clenched as she tried to rub the chill off her arms. The long-sleeved shirt she wore was still wet, and the outside temperature kept dropping. "Don't sugarcoat anything for my sake. I want to know what I'm up against."

"Okay. I promise to always tell you the truth.

Yes, it is a possibility. If he's smart, he'll stay away, but he could be out there, looking for us. All we can do this second is remain vigilant."

"And pray we're rescued before someone shoots us." She shuddered from both the cold and the all-too-familiar feelings of fear haunting her. While staring out into the forest, searching for danger, she jumped at every shadow flickering in the wind.

Minutes later, her vision turned hazy, and a memory returned.

Her mind floated back to yesterday morning— before she was running for her life. Although the sky was bright then, her mood was dark. She drove her metallic blue hatchback slowly through a neighborhood she didn't recognize. Keeping her eyes trained on two men down the street, she kept her distance, afraid to be caught…

Zach watched the waves of the splashing flood-water dip and roll like a roller coaster as it raced down the creek. Sirens that signaled the pursuit of the shooter had faded away. An encouraging sign. The chase was nowhere near them.

Still standing behind the tree, he inhaled the aroma of pine while studying the dense land-scape around them. Not seeing anything out of the ordinary, he checked on Janel, who sat on the ground beside his legs. The dazed expression on her face frightened him. His first thought was the frigid waters had aggravated her concussion. He crouched and placed his hand on her shoulder. "Janel, can you hear me?"

She jerked and looked up at him with dull, clouded eyes. "I remembered something."

That would explain the shocked appearance. Concerned about her emotional well-being, he sat and took her hand in his. "Do you want to tell me?"

After a quiet moment, she drew in a deep breath. "Yesterday morning, at least an hour before you found me in the forest, I sat in my car and watched two men in an old truck pulling a trailer filled with tree branches. I stayed far back at the street corner, where they were less likely to notice me."

"Why? Do you know them?"

She shook her head. "No. I don't even know why I was watching them."

"What did you see?" He noticed her hand was feeling warmer and color was slowly returning to her face. Talking appeared to be helping.

"The driver parked along the curb in front of a Victorian house, then he and another man climbed out of the truck."

Zach raised his brows. The shooting took place behind a Victorian. "What did these men look like?"

"The driver had red hair. He was lanky and wore jeans and a long-sleeved shirt with a logo.

I got the impression that he was in his late twenties, maybe early thirties. The other man wore black jeans and a…" Her gaze locked on Zach's. "A black hoodie that covered most of his face. He's the man who chased after me."

"A redheaded landscaper was shot and killed near the forest where I found you. He had a trailer attached to his white truck."

"The truck I remember was white." She shuddered, most likely from the cold, but possibly from anxiety, as well. "We thought I might have witnessed the murder, but it didn't feel real until now."

"This could be the traumatic event preventing you from recalling most of the past two days. Only…" He struggled to make sense of what he knew.

"Only what?"

"The shooting happened in the backyard, not the front. Did you park and follow these men?"

"I don't know. Maybe." She nervously bit her lip. "I'm not sure I can handle remembering a murder. I've never seen anyone die before. My mother passed away quietly during the middle of the night when Karla and I were both sleeping."

Zach cradled her chin with the palm of his hand, wanting her to trust that he was here for her. "You're stronger than you think. I've seen that truth many times already."

"Even if you're right, with two shooters wanting me dead, I'll need a strength greater than mine."

He squeezed her hand, knowing she meant God. "He'll see you through this, and so will I."

She placed her other hand on top of his. "Thank you. Thank you for being you and being here for me." After a brief pause, she looked up at him. "Zach, how did this shooter know we would be on this road?"

"That's a good question. Your ex would have known if his neighbor called him after talking to Cole, or Karla might have said something to Charlene while helping at the gallery."

Janel shook her head. "Considering the circumstances, I'm willing to consider the possibility that Todd might be involved in the burglary. He could have hired these shooters—but not Charlene. She wouldn't do this to me. To anyone."

The unexpected sound of an engine made them both jump to their feet.

Gun in hand, Zach spied around the tree trunk but couldn't see any vehicles. "Stay here. I'll check it out."

He could tell she wanted to protest, but she relented and nodded her understanding. When he left her, she was leaning against the tree, rubbing her arms. Their clothes were still damp, and the chill was bone deep.

Cautiously traveling along the grassy bank, Zach scanned his surroundings for the source of the engine noise. Near the bend, he spotted Cole and a deputy carrying a boat down the cliff on the opposite side of the creek. He wished there was a bridge, but rowing a boat was better than swimming.

Waving to his brother, Zach noticed the storm clouds were drifting even closer. He ran to Janel and grabbed her hand. "It's time to go home."

"Home…" Relief flickered over her face for a brief second. They both knew she would return to the ranch, not to her own house.

By the time they turned the bend in the creek again, Cole and the deputy were lowering the boat where the water appeared less treacherous and then took turns climbing inside. Zach placed his arm around Janel's damp back as they waited impatiently.

While the muscular deputy helped row, Cole barked orders each time the current took control and turned the boat downstream instead of across. Water splashed everywhere.

Once the boat reached them, Cole jumped out and Zach helped pull it up to the bank.

"It's about time you got here." Zach slapped his brother on the back.

"I've been a little busy." Cole smiled, then turned to Janel. "Ready?"

"As ready as I'll ever be." She waited for Zach to climb inside and reach for her hand. "Did I mention I'm not a boat person?"

"No worries. I've got you." He guided her to the middle seat.

Janel cringed as they rocked. "Now I remember why I don't fish."

"You're doing just fine." Zach sat protectively close to her while Cole pushed the boat back into the turbulent waters, then jumped inside.

They rocked furiously, and Janel grabbed hold of Zach's arm. He had to admit, if only to himself, he didn't mind.

Out in the open, away from the canopy of trees, the winds ushered in the storm. He clamped his teeth shut to keep them from chattering. Janel shivered. They both needed to change into dry clothes as soon as possible.

Lightning lit up the sky and thunder clapped thirty seconds later, which meant the rain was maybe six miles away. Zach kept a nervous eye on their surroundings. The water rushing around them picked up speed. The nearby storm dumped more rain into the creek. They needed to reach land before a flash flood drowned them all.

SIX

"Faster!" Zach used his hand to help row the boat through the frigid water. They worked hard to reach the opposite bank before the rising floodwaters had a chance to swallow every inch of flat, dry land, leaving them no place to run ashore. His lieutenant emerged from the path that led up the side of the cliff. He rushed to the water's edge and grabbed the boat's bow, allowing the deputy to disembark.

The two sheriff's officers fought against the fierce current to steady the boat while Zach climbed out, taking care not to send Janel flying overboard. With Cole's guidance, she shuffled up to the front.

When she reached out to him, Zach placed his hands on her waist and lifted her high into the air with ease before setting her down on the grass, away from the water's edge.

"This way." Lieutenant Yeager led them to the path while the deputy dealt with the boat.

Zach took one last look at his sinking SUV.

The water had reached the top of the windows and was splashing over the roof.

"We'll fish her out for you." Lieutenant Yeager stopped walking long enough to emphasize a point. "Cars come and go. The important thing is you two are alive, an amazing feat when you think about it. You evaded a motorcycle in a forest while driving an SUV."

"He's right," Janel said, smiling up at him. With her deep blue eyes, cheeks pink from the cold and strands of damp hair framing her heart-shaped face, she looked like a porcelain doll. "You saved my life—again."

Zach stared back at her in awe. By the grace of God, she had summoned the courage and strength needed to survive the harsh elements while still suffering from a concussion. "You swam like an Olympian."

A blush rose from her neck.

"Let's get going," the lieutenant said, yanking them out of the moment. "You two must be freezing."

After the brief climb, Yeager removed two emergency blankets from his official vehicle.

"Thank you." Janel wrapped the heat-reflective plastic sheeting over her shoulders and hugged it tightly to ward off the cold.

"Any update on this new shooter?" Zach asked his supervisor, while wishing he had warm clothes to offer Janel.

"We're bringing in a drone to assist in our search." Yeager scratched his bearded chin. "Did you get a good look at him?"

"Just enough to see he's bigger than the murderer who wore the black hoodie and had an average build. This guy is taller, looks like a football player, has light brown hair, wears aviator sunglasses, along with a camouflage jacket, and drives a black motorcycle."

"Cole passed on the information about his clothing." The lieutenant, a friend since the first search and rescue they worked together, walked a few yards away from Janel and waited for Zach to join him. "The background checks you asked for on the gallery's assistant manager and her boyfriend came back clean. No priors for either of them. Robert Matthews received an honorable discharge from the army ten years ago. Since then, he's been working in real estate."

Army? Zach lifted a brow. "Any special weapons training?"

"Only the usual. There's nothing in the report to suggest he's one of our guys."

"Ja… Miss Newman will be glad to hear her assistant manager's boyfriend doesn't have a wanted poster." Zach hoped his slip of the tongue, almost calling Janel by her first name, wouldn't prompt Yeager to ask how well he knew her. If he thought Zach was too close of a friend to remain objective, he might reassign a different deputy to safeguard her.

With nothing else to discuss, they rejoined the others in time to hear Cole telling Janel, "Your former boyfriend hasn't been to the RV park in months."

Confusion flickered through her expression. "Didn't you say he was planning to spend a few days there?"

"That's what his next-door neighbor told us."

"She would know." Janel pushed aside the strands of hair that fell in her face. "There's only one neighbor Todd talks to, and she watches his cat when he's away. He loves his tabby like a child and wants to be reached in case of an emergency."

Zach wondered if the neighbor alerted Todd to the fact the police were asking questions. "Janel, did you get a look at the guy shooting at us today?"

"Not a good one, but I know it wasn't Todd."

"Let's pick your sister up on our way to the ranch." Zach hated to interfere with her business, especially when he knew it was on shaky ground already, but safety came first. "You need to convince Charlene and Karla that their lives may depend on closing the gallery until we lock up these shooters."

"It's for the best," Lieutenant Yeager confirmed before turning to Zach. "Your phone is drenched, isn't it?"

"I'm afraid so." He noticed the dismay register-
ing on Janel's face and wished he could make this
all go away for her. She should be able to focus
on her business instead of running from gunmen.

Yeager sent a text message before announcing,
"A deputy will deliver a temporary phone and vehicle to the ranch."

"Thanks." Zach caught the scent of rain in the
air and felt a drop land on his cheek.

"I have the heater turned on high," Cole called
out, waving them over to his SUV.

"You don't have to tell me twice." The thought
of warmer temperatures put a spring into his step
as he escorted Janel to the vehicle.

Once inside, raindrops sprinkled the windshield, and the SUV's air vents blasted Zach's
body with a powerful wave of welcoming heat.
His skin tingled as the chill faded away. "Warm-
ing up back there?"

"Yes. Thank you." The stressors of the day
made Janel's voice sound shaky.

They drove to her gallery and found only
one parking space available. As soon as the car
stopped, she jumped out, leaving the blanket behind, and ran for the glass door. The deputy sitting in the sheriff's vehicle gave a nod when Zach
stepped out of the SUV. He returned the greeting.

Tugging the door open, Zach found Karla hugging Janel. Half a dozen customers cast quizzical
glances their way, obviously noting their dishev-

eled appearances. A gray-haired couple stopped flipping through the box of matted prints and spoke to one another in low voices, then left. A middle-aged woman finished paying for her purchase, then stepped outside with a man who carried shopping bags.

With the gallery appearing to be safe, Zach took notice of the missing art. When he was there to drop off fall festival materials, he had admired her mother's work. At least twenty Southwestern-themed paintings hung on the walls around the empty spots where the stolen paintings had once been the major attraction. White pedestals of various sizes now held colorful cowboy statues made of resin. They were nice, but nothing compared to the bronze VanZandts that were once displayed in the center of the room.

A tall, clean-cut man glanced at the badge clipped to Zach's belt and stepped forward to offer his hand. "Deputy, I'm Robert Matthews. I volunteered to keep an eye on the place while Janel is having…issues."

They shook hands, and Zach took notice of the man's firm grip, along with his dark blue suit and spicy cologne. "So, Mr. Matthews, you're Charlene's boyfriend."

"Please, call me Robert."

Zach nodded and turned to the petite young woman behind the counter. "Miss Owens, we spoke over the phone yesterday."

Charlene's expression switched from pleasant to troubled. "I wish it had been under better circumstances."

Cole entered, and the appearance of a uniformed law enforcement officer was enough to send the straggling customers out the door. He changed the sign from Open to Closed, and Charlene raised her brows.

Janel hurriedly told everyone what had happened. "With a second shooter to worry about, Karla and I need to go back to Walker Ranch, and...we have to close the gallery."

"No!" Charlene blurted, but then seemed to realize the seriousness of the situation. "Can we at least fulfill our online orders? A dozen came in this morning. Your friends, other gallery owners and collectors around the state, are doing what they can to help, namely buying artwork."

A long pause hung in the air, and Zach offered his opinion. "If you take what you need home with you, there shouldn't be a problem."

Charlene looked hesitant before asking Janel, "Are you okay with me taking paintings and supplies home before I mail them?"

"Of course." Janel's tone held no doubt. "If this gallery is going to survive, we need to work together."

"I'll help." Robert grabbed a roll of tape from a bottom drawer, then Charlene told him where to find the other mailing supplies. Together, they gathered what they needed to complete the orders.

Zach held the front door open while Robert carried a load out to his green Mercedes-Benz. Karla wrapped paintings for transport, and Cole handed them to Charlene's boyfriend when he returned.

Janel stared up at the blank spaces on the wall, and Zach's heart ached for her. He left the door to stand with her.

The last flicker of light dimmed in her eyes. "Seeing my mother's paintings gone is…heartbreaking."

"I'm here for you," Zach said. "No matter what you face." Remembering his ex, he added, "That's what friends are for."

She sent him a gentle smile.

He wanted to kick himself for adding the "friends" part. *Friends.* At this moment, it was Zach's least favorite word. He found it strange that he could risk his life tracking down and confronting murderers, but was unwilling to risk his heart on a rebound relationship.

Janel's eyes soon clouded over as she sat there, staring at the wall for what seemed like an eternity, but was maybe five minutes. She suddenly shook her head as if coming out of a daze. "I just remembered going to the bank yesterday." She glanced at her sister, who stepped closer. "I had to tell the loan officer about the burglary. Putting it off would only make me feel worse."

Karla nodded. "I get it."

Janel breathed in deeply, then exhaled. "I re-member crying at the loan officer's desk. She was sympathetic and gave me a box of tissues, but I felt like a blubbering fool."

"About that..." Karla's gaze traveled between Zach, Cole and Janel. Charlene and her boyfriend were working in the back room. "My friend from work called. Frank Hyde, the investigator as-signed to your claim, knows about your meeting with the bank and how you used the paintings as collateral to secure the loan."

"I wasn't hiding anything," Janel stated de-fensively. "I did the responsible thing. My loan papers said they could take the paintings if I de-faulted on the loan. Since I no longer had posses-sion of them, I needed to let them know I would turn over any insurance money I receive for the paintings. There was something to that effect in the loan papers. And if it isn't enough to cover what I owe, they'll put a lien on the gallery."

Karla placed a hand on her sister's shoulder. "We know you aren't hiding anything."

"Then what's the problem? Why are you look-ing at me like a two-year-old who spilled her milk on purpose?"

"I didn't mean to." Karla sighed. "Hyde already thought the burglary was an inside job because your security code was used to turn off the alarm. Once he heard you went to the bank right away, he immediately suspected insurance fraud. He thinks you stole the paintings so you would never lose them."

Janel's jaw dropped. "I…"

Charlene stood near the back door, her hands planted on her hips. "No one in their right mind could possibly believe you had anything to do with the burglary."

"He doesn't know Janel the way we do," Karla calmly explained.

"If I stole from my gallery, why are two men trying to kill me?" Janel asked, her tone incredulous.

Zach had his own theory. "Hyde might think you hired them to steal the paintings for you so the bank couldn't take them, and then you refused to pay for their services. They don't want the artwork. They want their money—or your dead body."

Janel's dizziness began to fade now that she'd showered off the grime from the floodwaters and eaten a few bites of Mrs. Walker's delicious stew. The warm bowl felt good in her hands.

Their small group had gathered at the dining room table. Karla sat next to her while Zach and his sister, Lily, occupied the seats across from them. Mr. and Mrs. Walker had already eaten and were attending to chores, while Cole had returned home to his wife. They had a house on the far end of the property.

An open laptop near Zach displayed security footage of the ranch. The largest box on the screen rotated through each camera every five seconds, giving you one expanded, in-depth view at a time. Seven smaller boxes showed partial coverage of what the remaining cameras filmed.

The view of the horses playing and exploring beneath a magnificent sunset provided a much-needed sense of calm to Janel's turbulent day. She sipped from the water glass, then placed it down next to her bowl. "Lily, thank you again for picking up clothes for us, especially the extra pair of boots. It will take at least a day for my other pair to dry."

"No thanks needed. It was a team effort." In her early thirties, the youngest Walker sibling, with her golden locks, high cheekbones and keen marksmanship skills, was a cross between a cheerleader and a Wild West gunslinger. "Once Jackson and his team determined your house was safe to enter, I just needed to grab Karla's bag and pack one for you, using the list your sister made for me."

"Where *is* Jackson?" Karla asked. "He's done so much to help, and I haven't even met him yet."

"You will." Amusement danced in Lily's eyes. "He drops by the house at least once a day for Mom's cookies. Since finding out they're expecting their first child, his wife, Bailey, is determined to improve their health by turning their pantry into a sugar-free zone."

"A baby. That's wonderful." Janel's smile faded when she remembered Jackson had also built a house on the property. "We shouldn't be here. It's dangerous for Bailey."

"She's staying in town with her best friend for the next few days." Lily reached for a biscuit. "With Jackson working all over Northern Arizona, she doesn't mind. It's like having an extended slumber party."

Guilt gnawed at Janel. "We need to find these shooters so your lives can go back to normal."

It would help if she could remember more about the past few days. She had to be certain that the insurance investigator's suspicions about her were wrong; she didn't hire burglars now seeking revenge. The brief memory of crying at the bank proved she was innocent. Didn't it? Frank Hyde would probably say she was acting. Everything in her insisted he was wrong. But...what if he was right?

Sales had continued to drop at her gallery no matter what she did to bring in more customers. It was only a matter of time before she would default on the loan and lose their mother's legacy. She had been so tired from the doubts, fears and loss of sleep that she was dragging herself into work every day. Could she have become desperate enough to search for someone who would involve themselves in a burglary-for-hire scheme? She pictured herself hanging out in seedy bars, sizing up the men who entered.

No.

Maybe...

I've always tried to follow the scriptures. Could I have strayed?

Dogs barking caught their attention. A cacophony of disturbing pops and crackles mixed with high-pitched horse neighs, followed by the sound of pounding hooves, forced Janel to her feet. "What is that?"

"I can't find anything on the security monitor, but it sounds like fireworks." Zach pushed away from the table and rushed toward the living room windows, with his sister close behind.

Karla peered at the laptop's screen. "The ranch is so big, there are blind spots in the surveillance coverage."

Mrs. Walker appeared in the hallway, hurriedly making her way to the front of the house. "Who set off fireworks in the pasture? They're scaring the horses."

"We don't know for sure." But Janel could guess. The loud crackling noises continued. She stood, watching everyone take action, wishing there was something she could do to help.

Zach removed a heavy-looking black gun from

his hip holster, and Lily opened a cabinet to retrieve a pearl-handled one with a long barrel.

"It has to be a trap," Janel warned. "He wants you to run out the door." The shooter must have followed them, somehow. The lump on her forehead throbbed so badly her eyes narrowed, and her stomach churned.

"We'll be fine." He touched her shoulder before heading out the door. "Stay here."

Mrs. Walker grabbed a rifle from the gun rack mounted to the wall. "I'll guard our guests."

Janel pointed to the laptop. "Karla, if you keep an eye on the surveillance footage, I can look out the window."

Mrs. Walker started to object but appeared to change her mind. "Stand to the side of that window near the corner, and I'll take this one."

Before getting into position, she prayed. *God, please grant us the courage and wisdom needed to fight these intruders. Amen.*

With two fingers, she widened the space between the cream-colored slats to peer outside. Across the ranch, bright lights exploded one after another as they stretched ten to twelve feet into the air. Fountain fireworks. She'd seen a similar display on Independence Day.

Making sure no one had sneaked up to the house, Janel's gaze swept over the porch. A white two-seater swing hung at her end. Two rocking chairs sat in front of the window, with a small wooden table between them. And a cast iron dinner bell was mounted to a wooden pillar near the steps. Nothing out of place or alarming there.

Next, she surveyed the surrounding area. Zach, Lily and Mr. Walker used the corner of the stables, piles of hay and a tractor as shields. But who did they need protection from? She didn't see anyone else. Seconds later, Cole and Jackson appeared from around a tree, guns ready. They must have heard the noise and come running from their homes.

"We have company out back!" Karla pointed to the laptop.

Mrs. Walker and Janel ran to the table to view the security footage. A man wearing camouflage and a ski mask held a gun in a ready position as he crept closer.

"I've got this." Mrs. Walker headed toward the back door.

No matter how good Zach's mother may be with a rifle, Janel couldn't let her face this shooter alone. There had to be a way to alert the Walker family all at once.

Remembering the dinner bell, Janel ran out the front door and yanked the chain back and forth. The loud, repetitive clang caught the attention of everyone on the ranch. She made eye contact with Zach, who took a step away from the stables.

"Behind the house!" She made a sweeping gesture. "Hurry!"

When he bolted in their direction, she ran inside and locked the door. Turning, she found Mrs. Walker standing in the center of the room, aiming her rifle at the closed back door in case the shooter broke in.

Karla stood in the hall entryway, holding a gun she must have borrowed, since she didn't have her own pistol with her. "Are you crazy going outside? You could have been shot."

"But I wasn't." Janel smiled, knowing it was something Zach would say. Peering into the laptop again, she could no longer see the intruder. Did that mean he fled when he heard the bell?

Or was he waiting for the Walkers to come closer?

Fear seized her heart. Did she just send Zach straight into a trap?

SEVEN

Scared senseless, Janel forced each breath into her body. She sat on the living room rug behind a wing-backed chair, her legs crisscrossed and her hands holding on to the open laptop. From her position, she could see Mrs. Walker, aiming the rifle at the back door, and Karla, standing in the hall, holding a gun. What she desperately wanted to see was Zach.

Finally, he appeared on the screen. Relief engulfed her. She hadn't sent him into a trap after all.

"Zach and Lily are moving toward the shed." Janel provided a play-by-play account of what she witnessed through the surveillance footage. She anxiously studied the screen, hunting for the masked man. What she would do if she spotted him was a question swirling through her mind.

"What about the others?" Mrs. Walker spared a quick glance in her direction before focusing on the rear entry of the house again. None of them wanted to be taken by surprise.

"Your husband is searching the cars parked near the house. Cole and Jackson jumped the fence where the fireworks went off and are running toward the trees. They must have spotted someone on that side of the ranch." Her chest felt heavy. The second intruder could be the murderer who chased her through the forest.

Janel noticed Mrs. Walker's arms were lower than before and suspected she couldn't maintain her guarded stance for much longer. "Do you want to trade places? I can hold the rifle while you watch the security footage."

"I'm fine." Mrs. Walker kept her eyes glued to the door, and Janel could see Zach in the woman's determination.

Karla sent Janel a grim smile. "Let's hope someone gets arrested today."

"Yeah." The last thing she'd wanted was for the ranch to be attacked. No one near her was safe, no matter where she hid. She checked the laptop screen at the exact second Zach started running away from the shed. Lily followed his lead. "I think they found the masked guy who tried to sneak up on us."

"What do you mean by 'think'?" Karla left her spot in the hallway to join her.

"Zach and Lily are running after someone." Janel pointed to the far end of the screen until she could no longer see them. "Mrs. Walker, your family has chased them off the ranch." Janel wanted to stop worrying but couldn't. These men kept showing up when least expected.

The older woman slowly exhaled a long breath before collapsing onto the sofa. She placed the rifle at her feet. "Just in case," she noted.

After ten excruciatingly long minutes, Zach knocked on the locked door.

Janel sprang to her feet and let him inside. "What happened?" She'd already seen him approaching on the laptop and knew that he and Lily had come back alone. "Did he get away? What about the other guy? Did Jackson and Cole catch him?"

"Yes, and no." Zach sat on the ottoman near his mother, but kept his gaze on Janel. "From the description Jackson gave me, it looks like our fugitive set off fireworks in the pasture to distract us."

"The murderer," Janel muttered.

Zach nodded. "Same black hoodie and mirrored sunglasses. He took off on an ATV parked on that side of the ranch. His buddy—"

"The guy who shot at us today. I recognized the camouflage jacket," Janel noted.

"Correct. He must have figured we would all run toward the fireworks and leave you unprotected."

"Silly man." Mrs. Walker guffawed. "He would have had a surprise waiting for him if he had tried to come through that door."

"That's right." Zach smiled at his mother. "Unfortunately, he had a head start and ran for the ATV he had parked on this side of the ranch."

Karla left the hallway and eased onto the sofa next to Mrs. Walker. "Zach, did your lieutenant find us a safe house yet?"

"We talked." Zach rubbed his chin with the pad of his thumb, thinking again. "They haven't found a safer place for you. No houses are available, and motels have too many people around. At least here we have three law enforcement officers living on the property, and the sheriff will increase patrols nearby."

As if on cue, sirens sounded in the distance. The response time out here was longer than she'd like. *Maybe that will improve now.* "I don't understand why they are so determined to kill me. I get that I might be able to identify the murderer if my memories return, but they could leave the state, or the country."

"I have a theory," Karla said. "If there are several people tied to the burglary and murder and they all suddenly move, it would be like advertising their guilt when you identify one of them."

"I hadn't thought of that." Janel turned to Zach. "What do you think?"

"She makes a valid point. They could also have a life here they don't want to leave, especially if they have influential careers, a lot of money or strong family ties." Zach's gaze shifted between the sisters. "You two would go to great lengths to protect one another."

"True." Janel recognized the sound of Lily's boots on the back porch. "Just like your family members protect one another."

The door swung open, and the conversation stopped as Lily entered the living room. "The deputies are taking statements. They'll come to the house soon."

Glancing at the laptop once more, Janel counted four sheriff's vehicles parked on the ranch. She wished she could tell them what the murderer looked like. Now that the most dangerous moments were over, her temples throbbed with the onset of another headache. The doctor had warned her to relax. That wouldn't happen until these men were caught.

"We have to get ahead of this," Janel announced.

Lines creased Karla's forehead. "Meaning what exactly?"

Looking Zach straight in the eyes as if she could bend him to her wishes, Janel stated, "I need you to take me to the place where the landscaper died."

"No." His tone held firm.

Karla huffed. "You want to go to a murder scene when masked men are trying to kill you?"

"It doesn't matter where I go, they'll keep trying." Frustrated, Janel bit her lip while she reined in her emotions. "Please try to understand. I need to do this. Zach and I both agree that witnessing the murder could be the emotional event blocking my memories. If I'm there, in person, everything might come back to me."

Lily turned to her brother. "This morning's shooting did trigger her memories of the landscaping truck."

Zach worked his jaw while he remained quiet.

Janel tried another approach. "We all need to get our lives back—sooner, rather than later. Keeping us here has turned your ranch upside down. Lily has had to move her horse riding lessons to other ranches. You can't book cowboy cookouts or hayrides while we're here. You must be losing business. I've had to shut my doors, so I know I'm losing business."

"Your life is more important than money," Zach shot back. "My entire family agrees with me on that."

"What he said." Karla gestured in Zach's direction.

Lily placed a hand on her brother's shoulder. "Zach, hiding here indefinitely could drag this out for a long time. Is that fair to Janel? She's the victim."

After what seemed like an eternity, he exhaled a long breath and relented. "If you're going to remember something important, it will most likely be where this all started. And I prefer to go on the offense, instead of defense. We need to bring Cole, since we all believe the killing and burglary are connected."

Karla crossed her arms over her chest. "I'm going with you, too."

Janel shook her head. "You need to stay here. If a shooter shows up, he might mistake you for me. Somehow, this is all my fault. I'm the one they're after, and I'm the one who must help catch them before someone else dies." Taking on the assertive sister role felt foreign to Janel, but good. She should do it more often.

"None of this is your fault," Zach insisted. "And even I know nothing short of a natural disaster is going to keep Karla from going with us." He removed his phone from his pocket. "I'm calling my lieutenant. If he gives our plan the green light, we'll need to prepare for anything that could go wrong."

The following morning, Zach drove a sheriff's vehicle up the mountain toward the high-end houses where the landscaper had been shot and killed two days ago. He still had reservations about this trip but knew they had to take steps toward ending the madness for everyone's sake. There was the ranch and his family to think about, as well as the twins' safety.

The tension in the cab grew thicker with every mile. Janel sat beside him, staring out the window, while her sister sat in the back, emailing contacts on her phone.

Karla huffed an exasperated breath. "According to my friend at the insurance company, Frank Hyde recently lost his biggest client. He needs a fast paycheck, so he formed an alliance with the detective working the burglary cases in Scottsdale."

"Frank, the insurance investigator who thinks I'm guilty?" Janel grimaced. "What type of alliance?"

"They're feeding each other information," Karla explained.

"That's not uncommon." Zach turned down a quiet residential road. "And it sounds like they think they're both trying to find the same burglars. As long as they follow the evidence, there shouldn't be a problem. In fact, this Scottsdale detective might convince Hyde that Janel had nothing to do with her gallery's break-in."

"Wishful thinking. Hyde molds the facts to fit his narrative." Karla leaned closer to the front seat and placed her hand on Janel's shoulder. "I won't let him smear your good name. We all know you didn't steal Mom's paintings."

Janel rubbed her temple, and Zach feared her memories of what happened the day before wouldn't come back if she was emotionally distraught over what Frank Hyde might do next.

Zach pulled up to the curb in front of the white

Victorian house. After parking behind Cole's SUV, he turned to his passengers. "My mother always says not to borrow trouble. Meaning, let's not worry about what hasn't happened yet. Instead, let's focus on the reason you convinced me to come here."

"You're right." Janel's tone was soft, almost apologetic, as she peered through the window at the stately looking house with blue trim. Two sheriff's deputies and Cole walked the property, ensuring the coast was clear.

"Wait here a minute." Zach scanned their surroundings before walking around the front of the truck to open the door for Janel and her sister. "I want you both to stick close to me or Cole."

"We will," Janel promised. While waiting on the sidewalk for her sister to climb out of the vehicle, she pointed to the asphalt in front of the mailbox. "The landscaping truck parked there Monday morning. I could see it from the corner."

Zach's gaze followed hers to the stop sign down the street. The shooting occurred at least eight hours after the burglary took place. If the two events are related, why did they come here?

She pressed her lips together while looking around. After a few seconds passed, she closed her eyes as if willing her memories to return. The three of them waited. And waited. When she swayed, Zach grabbed hold of her arm to keep her from falling.

Her lids flitted open. "The man in the hoodie and the redheaded one with him grabbed rakes out of the truck and walked that way." She pointed to the open area, at least fifty feet wide, between the Victorian house and its nearest neighbor, a house with a stone facade. Neighborhood doorbell cameras showed two men in the landscaping truck. The murderer had managed to keep his face hidden.

Zach had also learned from his lieutenant that the owner of the Victorian worked for an engineering company and was in Flagstaff when the shooting occurred. He told them the owner of the stone house was spending the holidays in Florida. Not a bad idea, considering the temperature here had dropped to where you could see your breath.

Afraid to break her train of thought, Zach remained silent as he followed Janel with Karla at his side. Cole walked toward the back of the two houses with the younger, taller deputy. The more experienced deputy staked out the front.

The decorative landscape between the houses included lush winter grass, manicured evergreen shrubs and beds of colorful flowers. Nothing seemed to trigger another memory; her blank expression remained constant.

Once she stepped into the clearing behind the houses, they could see the forest straight ahead, bordering both unfenced yards. A ladder at the corner of the Victorian stood beneath newly installed motion detecting lights. Empty boxes littered the grass next to both houses. If anyone returned at night, the area would light up like a football field.

Standing in place, Janel quietly looked around. Yellow caution tape tied to the Victorian's wooden porch posts stretched over the grass to the forest trees, blocking off the crime scene. A blood patch in the middle marked the spot where the landscaper was shot and killed.

Zach studied Janel, hoping for any sign of recognition. She turned toward the backyard of the stone house. Gray-colored covers protected the porch's outdoor furniture. Twenty feet away, Adirondack chairs surrounded a firepit. Her gaze appeared to lock on a casita, which might serve as a guesthouse or mother-in-law suite.

When Karla opened her mouth to speak, Zach raised a finger, stopping her. He wanted Janel to have uninterrupted time to take in the scene.

Cole and the deputy continuously looked out for trouble, reminding Zach of the danger Janel was in just standing here. A pang of guilt struck his stomach. This was a mistake.

"I followed a man with dark hair from Sedona," she blurted and strode straight toward the Victorian house. "I tried to remember why, but there's a mental wall blocking that memory."

Anticipation rose in Zach's chest. "Try to relax. It will all come back to you."

"Eventually," she said, despair hanging heavy in the air.

"We came here for you to remember." Karla took her sister's hand and pulled her away from Zach. "Think. Was the man with the dark hair the guy who chased you through the forest and blew up my car?"

Agitated by Karla's pushy interference, Zach clenched his jaw, but then he noticed Janel's wide eyes.

"Yes," Janel answered. "It was the same man. He drove a silver sedan up the mountain. When he reached the forest, he pulled off the road, onto the shoulder behind the landscaping truck and trailer. He covered his hair with a black hoodie before he climbed inside with the redhead."

"Then you saw his face?" Karla exclaimed.

"No, I didn't. He had his back to me."

Zach tipped the brim of his cowboy hat. "How did you not get caught following them?"

"I hid on the other side of a slow RV when I passed them, then I found a place to park and wait for them to drive by before following again at a safe distance."

"Do you remember the make and model of the silver car?" Karla rubbed her temple, concern flashing through her expression.

Janel shook her head. "You know I'm not into cars."

Zach stepped between the sisters to capture Janel's attention and gestured toward the backyard of the Victorian. "You were walking this way."

"Right." She ambled toward the porch, her expression one of deep concentration. "I... I didn't want them to see me, so I snuck closer and hid behind a tree."

"You parked and got out of the car?" Zach felt like he'd skipped a chapter in a book. He'd found her deep in the forest, far from this location.

"I must have." She touched the white railing surrounding the Victorian's porch on her way to the far side of the yard. Her pace increased until she reached a tree with a large trunk on the edge of the forest. She stepped behind it, then leaned out to face them. "I hid here, watching them."

Zach's gaze shifted from her to the bloodstain on the grass. She was roughly twenty feet away from where the landscaper was shot. "What else do you remember?"

Still gripping the tree, Janel closed her eyes. Soon, she gripped the trunk tighter, her arms shaking, sweat pooling at her brow. She sucked in a raspy breath.

Karla rushed over and pulled her sister into a hug. Janel cried on her shoulder.

Zach turned to his brother, whose expression showed empathy, but he stood back, silently watching. Cole must have felt as helpless as he did in the moment. Then he reminded himself that Janel wanted these memories to return. Nobody forced her. She was stronger than she looked—even now. He admired her for seeing this through.

When Karla glanced up at him, he said, "We need to know what happened next, while the memories are fresh."

Janel lifted her head. "It was horrible. I never saw anyone die so violently."

"I have. You're right. It's horrible. I'm sorry you were here when it happened." Zach tried not to think about the times he had to shoot another human, even if it was to help save his sisters-in-law.

Their gazes locked, emotionally connected by a similar experience.

Janel abruptly jerked around. "I remember parking on that street." She pointed away from the houses. "I cut through this part of the forest. When I got close, I only moved when they made noise, so they wouldn't hear me." She looked back toward the crime scene. "The redhead was a real landscaper. He was doing his job, raking pine needles. The dark-haired man wearing the hoodie played at it. At one point, he went back to the truck for a blue canvas bag."

"What was that for?" Karla asked.

"He didn't say anything to the redhead when he carried the bag over to the casita and picked the lock." She stared in that direction for at least twenty seconds.

When her breathing grew shallow, Zach took

a step forward. "You're doing a great job. You've got this."

Drawing in a deep breath as if to summon her courage, she continued. "After the door was open, the redhead pulled a gun out of his pocket. The guy in the hoodie shoved his lock-picking kit into his pocket and told the other guy not to do anything foolish."

Tears flowed down her face. "Before the redhead had a chance to say anything, the guy in the hoodie lifted the gun hidden in his pocket and shot. The redhead fell backward." Her gaze traveled between Zach and Karla. "I couldn't help it. I gasped. He saw me. I… I had to get away."

"And that's how you ended up running far into the forest," Zach concluded.

"I could hear him shooting behind me. I ran and ran and ran."

A click sounded nearby, and Janel gasped again.

EIGHT

Fear and anxiety twisted in Janel's gut as the back door of the stone house flew open. At the same time, Zach, Cole and Jackson reached for their holstered firearms, keeping their fingers on the handle grips.

A casually dressed middle-aged man stepped out onto the porch, clearly disturbed by the sight of armed law enforcement officers. "What's going on?" He eyed the deputy standing beside the firepit and added, "This is my yard. I heard the shooting happened next door."

"I know him. Mr. Allen is a regular customer." Janel's voice weakened as her confusion grew.

A dozen questions crossed her mind, starting with why would a murderer break into his casita yesterday?

"Do you have identification?" Zach asked, keeping his hand near his holster. "We heard you were in Florida."

"I was until a neighbor called about the shooting. I flew back here immediately to check on my property." Mr. Allen removed his wallet from his back pocket.

Cole checked his ID and nodded. "He's the homeowner."

"Janel, what's going on?" Mr. Allen's gaze traveled between the two sisters.

She didn't feel the need to point out she had a twin. Partly because most people assumed the truth when they saw them together for the first time, but mostly because she didn't know if he had a connection to the men trying to kill her.

Remembering the casita, Janel gestured in that direction, and Zach asked, "Mr. Allen, did you find anything disturbed when you checked your property?"

"Not yet. Why? Did something happen to my guesthouse?"

Zach urged the homeowner to go inside with a sweeping gesture. "You tell us."

Mr. Allen glanced at the caution tape in his neighbor's yard with a wary expression. "I'm granting you permission to search anywhere on my property that you like."

Wise decision. Janel wouldn't want to be the first person to venture inside when the door stood partially open. Who knew what waited for them?

"Stay here. I got this." Cole peered through a gap between the blinds in the casita's side window, then walked around to the front stoop and disappeared inside the small structure. He was most likely looking for a connection between the shooting and the burglary. After several long minutes, he emerged and asked Mr. Allen to join him. The homeowner looked reluctant but cooperated.

Standing next to Zach, Janel wrung her hands while Karla fidgeted with her phone for several minutes.

"That statue is not mine." Mr. Allen's loud voice filled the silence. "I have nothing to do with it being here."

Not his? Janel had to see the statue for herself. She rushed to the door with Zach at her heels.

"I'm coming, too." Karla fell into step behind them.

They stopped at the door, giving Mr. Allen room to exit. Janel entered the apartment-sized living room and took in the decor. The casita was smartly decorated with an off-white loveseat, chair and ottoman. In the center was a black coffee table. On top sat one of the stolen VanZandt statues: a bronze cowboy riding a bronco. Her jaw dropped open. "That's my…"

Cole nodded. "I recognized it from the photos."

Karla nudged her and pointed to the built-in shelves. Her other three VanZandts were all on display as if they belonged here. "They hid them in plain sight. This proves your gallery burglary is tied to the murder outside and the attempts to kill you."

"Mom's paintings…" Desperate for answers,

Janel found the bedroom. Above the white goose down comforter hung a painting featuring a field of daisies, one she'd never seen before. Spinning around, she realized the other walls were all blank. Despair fell over her. "Where are they?"

"Keep looking." Karla dropped to her knees and lifted the comforter to peer under the bed. "Not here."

Janel followed her lead and tugged open the other door in the room. The walk-in closet was nearly empty, except for a hotel-style robe hanging near the far corner. She flipped up the wall switch and a single bulb illuminated cylindrical objects stashed behind the robe.

"Don't touch anything. I need to handle potential evidence." Zach pulled a pair of gloves out of a pocket and slipped them on while she moved out of his way.

It took every bit of Janel's self-control to keep from snatching the cylinders and ripping them open. If the statues were in the living room, the paintings had to be close by. She craned her neck, trying to see into the closet.

Karla stepped closer, trying to get a look, as well. "Did you find the paintings?"

"I don't know. Maybe."

Cole joined them in time to watch Zach carry out two mailing cylinders, the type Janel used in her gallery. He set them on the bed and then pulled the plastic seal off the end of the closest tube. Tipping it ever so slightly, a roll of white glassine paper slid out.

"Let me." Cole, already wearing gloves, peeled back one end of the paper enough to reveal the corner of a canvas. His eagerness to reveal the painting lit up his eyes while her pulse soared.

Janel spotted the familiar rust-colored rock formation and teal blue sky featured on the canvas and sucked in a breath. "It's Mom's." She closed her eyes and prayed, "Thank You, God. I feared I would never see them again."

Overwhelmed with emotion, tears streamed down her face. Zach gently placed his hand on her back. She was appreciating the gesture of comfort when her sister ran to the closet.

"Don't touch!" Zach ordered. "Cole needs to transport the evidence to the police station. The burglary is his case."

"I know. I'm only counting," Karla called out from inside the door where they could still see her. Seconds later, she announced. "There are eight more. There should be ten cylinders, not nine."

"They might have rolled two paintings together," Zach suggested.

"I hope not." Janel wiped her face with her fingers. "That could crack the paint." Now that they'd found her mother's legacy, or at least most of it, she hoped they were all in pristine condition.

A deputy stepped inside the bedroom. "We located Miss Newman's car. It's parked around the corner, like she remembered. Halfway down the block between a truck and an SUV." He dangled her keys from the rhinestone heart-shaped charm attached to the ring. "These were in the grass and—"

"I must have dropped them." Janel accepted her keys from the deputy. He also held her burgundy-colored leather purse by the strap at his side, which triggered another memory. "I put my phone in my purse and shoved them both under the car seat before sneaking across the edge of the forest to spy on the landscapers."

After he handed over her purse, she dug inside for her phone and discovered the battery had died. That was probably for the best. If the movies she'd seen were correct, the murderer could use her phone to track her.

"Now that you mention it," Zach said, his tone hard. "Leave the surveillance to the professionals."

"Spying is illegal," Cole pointed out.

"I'm sure she learned her lesson." Karla reached for the keys. "I'll drive your car back to the ranch. You don't want to leave it here. And with that concussion, it's better that you don't drive yet."

An image of her sister being shot struck Janel like lightning. "No!" She held the keys to her chest. "You shouldn't drive my car. You look too much like me, and there are now two men who desperately want me dead."

* * *

"We can tow the car," Zach said, agreeing with Janel.

"There's no need for that." Karla huffed. "I'm an investigator, even if I do work for an insurance company. I've had to travel in crime-ridden areas and speak to people you wouldn't want to run into in a dark alley."

"Can you at least wear the hood of your coat to cover your blond hair?" Janel asked, her voice laced with annoyance.

"Sure, if it will make you happy, sis."

With that settled, Zach conferred with his brother. They decided Cole and one deputy would stay behind to transport the artwork to the police station, while the other deputy helped escort the sisters to the ranch.

Before leaving the casita, Zach pointed to the camera positioned in the living room corner near the ceiling. He was familiar with the model and knew a small red light should be glowing. "Cole, can you ask the homeowner which security company he uses and when this camera was turned off?"

"I already did. It was on when he left town, and I found no sign anyone tampered with the power source." Cole reached for his phone. "I'll text you the name of the company."

"Thanks." Zach was interested in knowing if this camera was shut off remotely without the homeowner being notified. If so, it would show Janel's break-in wasn't necessarily an inside job. He hadn't forgotten the technician who installed the gallery security system may have seen her enter her code and had skills worth investigating.

He wanted to prove her innocence, especially with the insurance investigator teaming up with the Scottsdale detective to make her look guilty. There was also Charlene to consider. She knew Janel was staying at his ranch.

In front of the house, Karla pulled up the coat's hood, hiding her blond hair. "See." She turned to Janel, modeling her new look. "I'm a giant marshmallow."

Janel rolled her eyes. "Please, be careful. And keep an eye out for a shooter."

"I will." Karla looked directly into her sister's eyes. "I promise."

The younger of the two deputies stepped forward. "I can drop her off at the car and stick close to her during the drive back." His tone was professional, but his expression showed he was eager to help. "If I see anything suspicious, I'll hit the siren." He lifted his finger, indicating one more thing. "And before she gets in, I'll check for any devices that shouldn't be there."

Bombs. He meant bombs. The burglars had access to them. A fact they needed to keep in mind.

Janel handed the deputy her car keys, accepting his help. Karla waved and then followed the law enforcement officer to his sheriff's vehicle.

Janel watched them leave. "I wish she would drive back with us."

"We'll be close behind her." Zach admired the way Janel always looked after other people, but the truth was no one was 100 percent safe with two shooters out there—somewhere.

While tugging open the passenger door of the truck for Janel, he heard the soft whir of a helicopter. Peering into the cloud-filled sky, he spotted a blue aircraft. He knew the markings for law enforcement copters. This wasn't one. Maybe a news crew. He hurried his efforts to leave before it flew closer.

His seat belt locked with a click, then he inserted the key into the ignition.

Janel reached over and touched his hand. "There's something I need to tell you."

"Can it wait?" He started the engine and turned on the heat.

"You might want to share what I have to say with Cole before we leave."

What now? Another memory? He leaned back against his seat and waited for her to explain.

"Mr. Allen recently bought a painting from my gallery. He asked Charlene to have it shipped to his house in Florida."

"Did you hear this conversation?"

She nodded slightly, and he began to understand her troubled expression. "Did he tell Charlene that he was going to be out of town for a while?"

"For two months." She pressed her fingers against her forehead. "I know this might make us both look guilty of stealing the artwork and hiding it here, but anyone in the gallery at the time could have overheard him."

"Not just 'anyone' knows your password." Something else came to mind. "Does your security footage also record audio? The security technician might have heard Mr. Allen say he wouldn't be home."

"Not to my knowledge. Do you have a tech team who can figure that out?"

"We have access to one." He let out a long breath, hating to see the toll every twist and turn was taking on her. "You're right, I need to speak to Cole."

She nodded again, then waited while he made a quick call to his brother.

Snow dusted the windshield during his conversation. At least it wasn't another downpour. He was tired of the rain. Before he shifted into gear, he turned to her one more time. "Thank you for trusting me with this information."

"I don't want to keep any secrets from you. Plus, I thought it would be better for everyone concerned if it came from me."

"True, but I know you don't want Charlene suspected of any wrongdoing."

"She's proven to be trustworthy time and time again."

When Janel turned to stare out the window, he made a U-turn on the residential street without expressing his thoughts on the subject. Many people, even trustworthy ones, have committed crimes when faced with dire circumstances. He needed to know more about Janel's assistant manager.

Down the street, Zach spotted the deputy turning right out of the residential neighborhood at the stop sign. Karla followed the deputy in an older model dark blue hatchback, only she ignored the stop sign.

Janel groaned. "I asked her to be careful."

"Does she always disregard traffic laws?" Zach slowed near the corner, stopped, then followed the others onto the main street leading to Sedona.

"Not *always*."

He let the subject drop as he centered his car in the right lane, thirty feet behind Karla. The deputy traveled in the parallel lane on her left side. A grassy median separated them from cars traveling in the opposite direction.

While driving downhill, Zach kept to the forty-five-mile-an-hour limit, and the gap between him and Karla grew. To his surprise, she surpassed the deputy. Speeding tickets must mean nothing to her.

"Slow down, Karla," Janel said, as if her sister could hear her. But Karla's speed increased with each passing second.

"I think there's something wrong." Zach flipped on the siren and pressed down on the gas pedal.

Suddenly, the emergency lights on the hatchback flickered a warning. Karla sped faster toward the red traffic signal at the bottom of the hill, where a busier street crossed their path.

Janel gripped the truck's grab handle. "There's something wrong with my car."

"Could be the brakes." Zach felt his pulse racing as he shifted into the left lane behind the deputy, who flipped on his siren and drove ahead of Karla, hopefully to block the intersection.

"Do something! Please." Desperation punctuated Janel's words. "She'll crash."

Zach suppressed the emotions Janel's screams brought on and concentrated on the situation. He sped up, closing the gap between them and the hatchback. He grabbed his phone from the cup holder and used facial recognition to unlock it for Janel. "Call Cole."

He tossed her the phone, then pulled up beside Karla and honked.

She pointed down, shook her head and yelled, "No brakes!"

Every muscle in his body tensed. He didn't need to hear her to know what she was saying. With little time to act, Zach laid on the horn repeatedly. Between his horn and the sirens, the drivers up ahead sped out of the intersection, which was about two hundred feet away. The deputy was almost there.

"Cole, it's Janel. The brakes are out in my car. Karla's in danger. We need help!"

With his pounding heart pummeling his chest, Zach searched their surroundings while Janel continued speaking to his brother. If her brakes had been cut, a shooter might be hiding nearby.

The windshield wipers swept away the snow with a loud swoosh, and more sirens sounded nearby. Most likely Cole and the other deputy.

A hundred feet from the intersection, drivers coming from the other direction eased off the gas and began to slow. He hoped their light was yellow and would soon turn red. They might avoid a crash after all.

The deputy entered the intersection and stopped, lights flashing and sirens blaring.

Despite the warnings, a brightly painted preschool van filled with young children didn't slow. The driver entered the intersection and abruptly stopped in front of the deputy, blocking Karla's path forward.

Zach instinctively threw his hand out in front

of Janel to protect her as he pressed hard on his brakes.

But Karla had no brakes.

With his breath caught in his throat, he watched in what looked like slow motion as Karla made a sharp right turn before reaching the intersection, avoiding a horrific collision with the preschool van. The hatchback flew over the curb, turned upside down and then landed in a ditch with a loud *thwack*.

Janel screamed. "No!"

Red and blue lights flashed in the rearview mirror. Cole was behind them. He could take care of Karla. Zach's job was to protect Janel. Without saying a word, he drove to the intersection where he turned right to avoid the preschool van.

"What are you doing?" Janel turned to look for her sister. "Go the other way! She could be dead!"

"Cole and the two deputies will take care of her. I have to get you out of here. A shooter might be watching."

"No!" She made quick work of unbuckling her seat belt. "You wouldn't desert your family. Don't expect me to desert mine." She pushed open the door as he slammed on his brakes. They both jerked forward.

"Are you crazy?" He reached across the seat to grab hold of her arm, but she jumped out of the car and ran back to the ditch where her sister had landed.

NINE

Janel sprinted down the sidewalk, her gut twisting into knots while she prayed her sister was alive. She ignored the pain in her forehead, made worse by sirens closing in, as she focused on reaching the car that had flipped over before landing. If there was a shooter nearby, she'd have to outrun his aim.

After jumping over the curb, she scurried over rocks and down into the ditch. Her boots slipped on the snow, and she gasped as she fought to regain her balance. Steady on her feet again, she rushed toward Karla, who lifted her hand and waved out of the open window.

The second Janel knew Karla was alive, a wave of overwhelming emotion swept over her, threatening to knock her off her feet. But nothing could stop her from reaching her sister, not even Zach and Cole, who kept calling out her name as they ran toward the crash site.

"I'm here." Janel fell onto her knees in the snow

beside the upside-down car and grabbed her sister's hand.

The seat belt and airbag pinned Karla in place. The windshield had shattered on impact, and the metal front end of the car had bent inward when it collided with the ditch's dirt and rock wall. "I'm sorry," she mumbled.

"It's not your fault. Are you okay?" Janel's throat burned as the words escaped, and her body sucked in much-needed air. "Does anything hurt?"

"I don't know." Karla sounded weak and scared. "I think I'm in shock."

"Don't move her," Zach warned. "Paramedics are on the way." He glanced about, reminding her of the potential for more trouble. If guns fired from uphill, they'd have to hide behind the car—if they weren't shot first.

"I'm not going anywhere." Karla coughed, then added, "I'm starting to feel pain in my wrist. The airbag hit my hand."

Cole hurried around to the passenger window and peered inside. "I don't see any obvious injuries or blood. That's a good sign."

The two brothers checked out the car, which took Janel's attention away from her sister until Karla spoke. "I should have listened to you."

That was a first. "Can I have that in writing?"

Kara chuckled, then groaned. "Don't make me laugh."

A fire engine and ambulance arrived, and Zach helped Janel to her feet. "We need to get out of their way."

He kept his arm around Janel as they walked over the uneven, snow-covered ground toward a tree growing outside of the ditch. "This is all my fault," she said, watching her step. "I should have insisted we tow the car."

"You were never going to win that argument with her."

Janel sniffled, refusing to cry again. "You pegged her right. She'll wear you down to get her way. I've let her do it too many times."

He pulled her close to his side when the fire-fighters descended on the scene and worked on freeing her sister from the car. Feeling light-headed, Janel turned away. "Zach, were my brakes cut? You and Cole checked my car."

"It looks like someone punctured the line. From what I can gather, most of the brake fluid didn't flow out until after the car was in motion."

He watched over the scene as she leaned her head against his arm. Her sister almost died again because of her. She dared to look. The paramedics were carrying a stretcher to the car. That meant a trip to the hospital. The possibilities spun in her head as the winter cold made her shudder.

"I didn't expect anyone to cut the brakes," Zach said, breaking into her thoughts. "They didn't come back for the artwork, which should have been their top priority."

"Mr. Allen came home, neighbors were on alert and I assume deputies were patrolling the murder scene. My car was around the corner and halfway down the block."

"True. But they should have stayed away. It was in their best interest."

"Their top priority is killing me. Why? He had that hoodie on and sunglasses. I never got a good look at the murderer's face."

"That you remember."

He was right. There was still so much locked away in her mind. She fought to regain those lost memories as the emergency responders lifted Karla onto the stretcher.

With guilt and fear at war to control her emotions, Janel rushed toward the closest paramedic, a tall man wearing a stoic expression. "Is she going to be all right?"

"I'm okay," Karla answered for him as they carried her toward the ambulance. "The only thing that hurts is my wrist. There's nothing to worry about."

"We're taking her to the hospital for testing," the paramedic explained. "Do you want to go with her?"

"No." Karla's tone was defiant. "Stay away from the hospital. Remember the last time?"

The bomb. Janel's gaze instinctively drifted to

the hills surrounding them, searching for a reflection of light that would reveal a shooter waiting to attack. "But…"

"You know I'm right." Karla's voice faded as they carried her away.

Janel jogged to catch up. "I'll call to check in on you."

"She'll be fine," Zach assured her. "God is looking out for her."

He was right. She could feel it in her heart. "Can a deputy go to the hospital with her?"

Zach nodded. "I'll make it happen."

Cole walked up, phone in hand. He ended his call and announced, "The insurance investigator is waiting for you at your gallery. He's insisting he speak to Janel."

Dread settled in her gut. "How much worse can this day get?"

Once they reached Sedona, Zach glanced over at Janel's waning features and decided a pit stop was in order. He turned the sheriff's vehicle toward his favorite drive-through restaurant. "I don't know about you, but I need a pick-me-up."

"Can we? The investigator is waiting for us." She straightened, taking an interest in the building with brightly colored posters of burgers and fries.

"Let him wait." Zach's chief concern was Janel's welfare. She'd been beaten down at every turn but still kept going. Aside from keeping her safe, he planned to support her by keeping her energy up. "We'll listen to what he has to say when we're ready and not a minute before."

A faint smile appeared on her beautiful face. "I like the way you think. And thank you. Something to eat sounds good."

After receiving their order, Zach parked beneath a tree away from the street, making them less likely to be noticed by drivers passing by. With the snow falling, the traffic was lighter than usual. He took a sip of his soda, then lifted his phone. "I got the impression your sister doesn't like this insurance investigator. We should learn more about him."

"How?" She glanced up from the drink she held with both hands.

"The internet." He entered the man's name in his phone's search engine and found a website. "Frank Hyde is an independent private investigator who offers his services to big corporations. He used to be a Phoenix police officer."

"Is that good or bad?"

"It depends on how he uses his training. I know someone who might have worked with him." He sent a text to his high school friend asking about Hyde.

"Can you also call the hospital to check on Karla?"

"It's too soon for test results, but I can give her

phone number to Lily. She can make calls while we meet with Hyde at the gallery."

Zach wasn't sure if Hyde's name brought on the angst in Janel's features or the fact she didn't know the extent of Karla's injuries. Maybe both. "What's your sister's phone number?"

He sent the text right after she rattled off the digits.

Lily replied right away. "Lily says she heard about the crash and is sorry it happened. And she'd be happy to help by keeping tabs on Karla and bringing her back to the ranch when it's time."

"Thank her for me." Janel stopped eating after three bites and stared at the traffic. He couldn't blame her for losing her appetite. She faced one challenge after another, and there was only so much he could do to help. Something he hated to admit since he was usually a problem solver.

Zach's phone rang. His friend was calling instead of texting. "Nick, how's it going?"

"The kids are keeping me busy, but that's not what you want to know," Nick said. "I heard about the shootings up there, and if Frank Hyde is involved, I feel sorry for you."

"Why? Does he have criminal ties?"

"Nothing like that, but he's a pit bull. He's quick to make judgments and sticks to them even when the facts say differently. He left the force after two years because rules didn't suit him."

Zach loathed the sound of that. The pit bull

had decided the gallery burglary was an inside job. "Does Hyde step over the line where rules are concerned or jump over it?"

"He straddles the line while he manipulates other people into breaking rules, laws, norms... you name it. It's only when he can't find anyone to do his dirty work for him that he'll break a law or two. He's smart enough to make sure he covers his tracks."

"What kinds of laws?"

"I hear breaking and entering is his favorite."

Zach caught the worry on Janel's face. "This will help. I owe you."

"And I'll collect one day. Good talking to you." Nick ended the call, and Zach let Janel know what he'd learned.

She pressed her lips together while she considered the news. "Hyde's worse than Karla thought. At least we know what he's like and it won't come as a surprise."

"Are you ready to meet him?"

"No, but we should get this over with." She took a long sip of her soda through the straw, then placed it in the cup holder.

Zach turned the key in the ignition and shifted the truck into gear. He couldn't help but check on Janel often during the drive through town. He cared about her deeply, but he needed to keep his feelings in check. Besides not wanting to risk his heart by playing the role of rebound guy again, he also couldn't be positive Janel hadn't participated in the burglary. Everything in him wanted to believe in her, but he had been wrong about a woman before.

The only vehicle parked in front of the gallery was a black Mercedes-Benz with darkly tinted windows. Zach left three spaces free between them and expected Hyde to emerge from the car. Instead, the gallery door opened, and Charlene ran outside.

Janel rushed to meet her halfway. "What are you doing here? You're supposed to be at home."

"Please don't be angry." Charlene's sweeping gaze included Zach in her plea. "A big order came in and the money was too good to let it slip from our hands, so Robert and I came back for the paintings and shipping supplies. We parked his Mercedes around back in case one of the bad guys drove by."

"And the insurance investigator showed up," Zach concluded. He wasn't thrilled with the idea that Charlene was here. He had hoped to keep the two women separated, but he might as well question her while he had the chance.

"Frank Hyde. He's inside." Charlene grimaced and gestured toward the door. "I already showed him where the stolen art was kept. He's not what I would call a pleasant man."

"I'm not upset that you're here." Janel sounded worried, though. "But next time, I would like you to call me first. Zach can arrange protection, right?"

"Sure." For a limited time. He held the door open for the women. "So, Charlene, do you live close by?"

"About five miles away." She waited for Janel to enter before she followed. "I did have a roommate, but she moved back to Phoenix. I haven't found anyone to replace her yet."

Zach made a mental note to finish their discussion later when he spotted a man standing on a step stool, examining a security camera in the corner. He wore a black T-shirt beneath a gray suit jacket. The kind body builders wore when they wanted everyone to see their muscles outlined by the form-fitting material. "You must be Frank Hyde."

"I am." He climbed down and took in Zach's badge clipped to his belt. "And you must be Deputy Walker."

"I am," Zach mimicked the man, whose attitude was living up to his reputation.

Charlene slid over next to her boyfriend behind the cash register counter and appeared to keep busy while obviously listening to the conversation.

Hyde took in Janel's disheveled appearance. "Miss Newman, I'm here on behalf of your insurance company to investigate your claim. I heard about your sister's accident. Someone else will contact you regarding your vehicle after you file that claim."

When no condolences or well wishes for her sister were added, Janel explained, "The car can wait. My sister's health is my primary concern."

"How noble of you. Detective Walker said someone punctured your brake line." Hyde removed a notebook from his back pocket. "Whose idea was it for your sister to drive your car?"

"Karla's," Zach snapped. Did the guy think Janel tried to kill her sister? "I understand you know her."

"I do." Hyde scowled.

"Then you know no one can talk her out of an idea when she's made up her mind." Zach walked closer to Janel. An unspoken message that he was on her side.

After opening the notebook, Hyde pinned Janel with his stare. "According to the security company, your password was used to shut off the alarm."

"They did say that," Janel admitted, "but there's a chance the man who installed the system watched me enter my password."

His expression turned smug. "But he wouldn't have known your customer was going to be out of town, offering the perfect place to hide the stolen art."

Zach shook his head in disbelief. "How do you know all of this about Mr. Allen?"

"The detective, your brother, if I'm not mistaken—and I rarely am—gave me the address where the art was found. I contacted the owner while I waited for you to arrive."

"The security technician might have an audio hookup here," Zach offered.

Hyde pointed to the camera. "Not up there."

"I'll have the place swept for bugs."

"You do that." He glanced down at his notes again. "Miss Newman, who knew your security code?"

"I created the code." Janel pressed her lips together as if wishing she didn't have to answer his questions.

"And then she shared it with me." Charlene's tone held no fear. "But I didn't steal anything." She looked at Janel apologetically. "Her old boyfriend, Todd, never turned his eyes away when she entered it into the panel."

Hyde lifted a brow. "Did Todd know Mr. Allen would be out of town?"

"No." Janel shook her head. "We broke up a month ago."

Hyde's gaze landed on Charlene's boyfriend. "What about you? Do you know the alarm code?"

Robert pointed to himself. "Me? No. I mind my own business."

"He always gives me privacy when I turn the alarm on and off." Charlene smiled at her boyfriend.

Hyde took down Robert's name, his occupation as a real estate agent and how often he was at the gallery. Then he asked Janel, "I heard there was a shooting next door to Mr. Allen's house yesterday, and the perpetrator chased you into the forest." He quickly explained to Zach, "Detective Walker filled in some of the missing pieces for me."

Janel pressed her lips together again. "Today, I remembered seeing the shooting."

"And that brings us to your amnesia," Hyde said. "Some people might think it's convenient you lost your memory. You can't tell the police why you were at the exact location where the missing art was found."

"That's enough!" Zach's ire was boiling over.

"I never said she was making up the amnesia. I've only been asking questions. Some of the other store owners on this block find the timing of your burglary odd." He sent Janel a smug look. "They say you've lost customers to a bigger gallery." He checked his notes again. "The bank manager said you were two weeks late with your last loan payment."

Janel's face turned red. "We found the artwork. Why are you even here?"

"According to the detective, there's still one painting missing. The most expensive one." Hyde stepped closer. "Did you know insurance fraud is a serious crime?"

"Get out!" Zach gestured toward the door. He'd

file a complaint with the insurance company contracting Hyde's services first thing in the morning.

"I'm not saying Miss Newman stole anything. I was wondering if someone might have done it for her. Someone who didn't want her to lose her mother's paintings." He glanced at Charlene, whose eyes grew wide.

"Out!" Zach repeated, wondering if the investigator was purposely being obnoxious to judge their reactions—who looked guilty and who didn't. Or was he taking out his dislike of Karla on her sister?

Hyde strode to the door. Before exiting, he announced, "Throwing me out will not stop me from doing my job. And until I'm convinced that this isn't an inside job, you won't receive one red cent." He took one last look around. "Nice gallery. It's too bad you aren't open for business."

Zach fisted his hand at his side. He'd met men who tested his patience before, but this one was upsetting a woman he cared for, making it twice as hard to control his temper. If the reports about Hyde were correct, the investigator would do everything he could to convince the insurance company that Janel or Charlene hired the burglars. Then there was Hyde, teaming up with the Scottsdale detective. Would they try to blame one of these women for the other burglaries, as well?

A nagging voice reminded Zach he couldn't

be positive they were innocent. He had trusted a woman who ran off with her ex. That reminded him they still didn't know if Todd was behind the burglary. Was he hiding? Would Janel go back to him if he declared he did this to show his love for her? The questions never stopped. Neither did the danger. It lurked around every corner.

TEN

When the door shut behind Hyde, Janel latched on to Zach's arm. "This situation is hopeless. I can't save my gallery unless I keep it open. And I can't do that unless you arrest those murderous burglars and prove they acted on their own. So far, you can't identify them to make those arrests unless I recall the memories I've lost."

"The doctor said you need to relax if you want to remember," Charlene added. A hint of embarrassment flashed across her face when they glanced in her direction. "Karla told me."

"Who can relax with a target on their back?" Janel ran her fingers through her hair. "I'm going to lose everything."

Zach placed his hand gently on her shoulder. "Let's get you to the ranch. My mother's hot tea and a night away from the chaos will do you a world of good."

"You're probably right." She was finding it almost impossible not to obsess over the troubles she faced every waking minute of the day. "Charlene, please lock up as soon as you're finished here. And don't take too long. I need you to stay safe."

"I promise to hurry." Charlene handed her boyfriend a stack of mailing labels. "Let's make sure we have everything on the list I printed."

"Just point me in the right direction." Robert turned to Janel. "We'll do everything we can to help. You only need to name it."

"Thank you. I will." On the way to the sheriff's vehicle, the snow crunched beneath Janel's feet. The cold chilled her to the bone, forcing her to shove her hands into the pockets of her coat.

During their drive, Zach turned up the heater, then asked about her phone. "I think we should charge it to see if you've received any threatening calls."

The possibility hadn't occurred to her. "If so, could they be traced?"

"It's a possibility. Also, voice analysis and background noises might help us find them."

For the first time, she felt a glimmer of hope. "I'll need a charger."

"We have plenty."

After what seemed like a long drive, they turned onto the ranch. She took in the sight of horses frolicking in the pasture, and a smile tugged at her lips. Maybe she could unwind for a few minutes.

Cole met them inside the garage. "How was your meeting with Hyde?"

Zach pushed the driver's side door closed. "He's pretending he hasn't already mentally tried and convicted Janel of burglary."

"That was the impression I got when he called to set up the meeting." Cole shifted his attention to Janel. "I hope he didn't get to you."

"How could he not?" Anger aimed at Hyde twisted in Janel's gut as she rounded the front end of the car. "He's blocking my insurance payment. If I default on my loan, the bank will take the paintings we found. And if I don't have the money for the missing painting, then the bank will put a lien on my gallery. I'm at my wit's end." So much for relaxing.

"We'll do whatever it takes to uncover the truth." Inside the kitchen, Zach removed a charger from a drawer and handed it to her, then hung his coat on the back of a wooden chair.

"Thanks." She placed her purse on the quartz countertop and dug inside for her phone. She plugged it in, then hung her coat on the back of a chair and sat while Zach turned on the gas burner beneath the teakettle.

Cole grabbed a water bottle from the fridge and joined her at the table. The laptop displaying the ranch's security footage was open next to him. "Lily and Mom left ten minutes ago. They're headed to the Flagstaff hospital to pick up Karla."

Finally, some good news. "That means the tests came back okay, right?"

Cole nodded as he swallowed a sip of water. "Aside from a sprained wrist and a multitude of scrapes and bruises, she's fine. She tried to call you, but your phone was dead. I told her you were meeting with Frank Hyde."

Janel would have trouble believing her sister was "fine" until she saw her in person. "When will they be back?"

"My best guess is a couple of hours. It's about a sixty-minute drive each way in the snow. They thought it best to go together. Mom can guard the car against bombers while Lily runs inside to collect Karla."

"No one should have to live like this," Janel mumbled. Glancing into the dining room, Janel noticed the blinds were down. They always covered the windows when she was here. No doubt to keep anyone from shooting at them. Again, she felt guilty for disrupting their lives and putting them in danger.

Zach had tried so hard to turn the ranch around after the local resorts turned to neighboring ranches for hayrides, cowboy cookouts and trail rides for tourists. They couldn't bring visitors onto the property with a targeted witness here. And after so many shoot-outs, how could they rebuild? They might all lose their livelihoods.

The key to ending this nightmare, for everyone's sake, was to remember what the murderer looked like. With fatigue settling in her bones, she rubbed her temples, wishing she could snap her fingers and have her memory back. *If only...*

"I haven't seen Dad," Zach noted. "Where is he?"

"Dusty is limping. The veterinarian agreed to squeeze him into his schedule."

"Horse?" Janel asked, trying to stay up with the conversation.

"Dog," the brothers answered in unison.

"That poor little fellow." Janel always wanted a dog but was never home long enough to take care of one.

The kettle whistled, and Zach opened a box of tea bags. "I guess it's just the four of us for a while."

"Three," Cole corrected. "Jackson is having dinner with Bailey. After last night, she's worried about him, and he wants to calm her nerves. Stress isn't good for her pregnancy. Once she's feeling better, he'll come back to help stable the horses."

"Jackson, a father..." Zach grinned. "That I have to see."

Janel felt she could relate in a small way to Bailey's fears. She wasn't married to Zach, or even dating him, but she worried something would happen to him every time he confronted the shooters. "I don't blame her for being concerned. Jackson should stay home with her. We'll manage."

"You're right. We will." Zach placed the bottle of creamer on the table. "The sneak attack last night failed, so they know we'll be keeping an eye out for them. Plus, there's increased patrol by the deputies on the main road leading to the ranch. You're safe. Focus on relaxing." He handed her a mug. "I hope you like chamomile."

"It's just what I need. Thank you." After half an hour, the laptop screen showed the sun disappearing below the horizon. Janel walked to the kitchen counter and checked at least thirty text messages with her phone still plugged in. Many were from Charlene and Karla on the day she hadn't returned to work. Seeing her ex's name made her stomach flip-flop. "Todd called and texted after he heard a murderer tried to kill me. He wants me to reconsider his offer to reconcile so he can protect me."

Zach worked his jaw, clearly agitated. "Did he say where he's staying?"

"His best friend is getting married, so he took time off work to drive to Colorado for the wedding."

"And didn't tell the cat sitter?" Zach shook his head.

Cole studied his brother's reaction, then turned to Janel. "Do you mind if I use your phone to call Todd?"

"Not at all." She stepped away from the counter. "While you have it, please check for any threats. I prefer someone else reads them."

"Will do." Cole unplugged the charger and carried the phone out of the room, leaving Janel to wonder what he might find.

"How do you feel about Todd texting you?" Zach's tone sounded flat, hard.

"I wish he hadn't." The anger and embarrassment brought on by the breakup stirred inside. "It's a reminder of how gullible I was. Someone I trusted betrayed me. And now, no matter how badly I want to believe it will never happen again, I can't help but wonder."

They sat quietly, sipping their tea, while studying the security footage on the laptop as the largest picture flipped from one camera view to the other every five seconds.

The pounding of hooves and frantic neighs jerked them out of their quiet thoughts. A small picture in the corner of the laptop showed light flying through the darkening sky. Zach double-clicked to enlarge that camera view. Flaming arrows, one after another, landed on the hay inside of a trailer. She couldn't believe her eyes.

"Fire!" Zach jumped to his feet.

Janel's entire body stiffened with fear. "They're here."

Cole ran back into the room and glanced at the security footage. "The fire is too close to the stables. I have to put it out."

"Watch out for the guy shooting arrows. And take a different route across the ranch. Last night, they learned how we react to danger and now they're escalating their attack." Zach pulled on his coat. "I'll deal with whoever thinks they're sneaking up to the house again."

Cole grabbed a coat and rushed to the living room.

"This can't be happening again. Nothing deters them." Watching the flames on the screen fueled Janel's anger. "And I've had enough of this!"

"Good." Zach opened the gun cabinet. "I need to go outside and stop them from setting fire to the house." He handed her a weapon. "If anyone gets past me, shoot him." He headed to the back door. "Lock up after I leave and call 911."

The second after Zach fled outside, Janel pulled the door closed and secured the dead bolt. She turned and faced the empty room. Standing still and listening, the silence grew deafeningly loud. Last night, Karla and Mrs. Walker had been here with her.

She refused to let fear consume her again. Lifting the cold, hard gun, her determination set in. "I won't let them kill me."

Peering out between the blinds, she called 911 and reported the situation while watching Zach. He scanned his surroundings as he inched toward the far end of the porch, climbed over the railing and jumped down. When he stepped out of sight, her heart hitched, and she prayed he would come back to her, safe and sound. And not just because he kept her alive time and time again. She wanted to be near him. Maybe one day, she'd trust her instincts again, and let herself fall in love. Maybe…

The automated floodlights turned on, bathing the yard in a bright glow. Aside from Zach, there was no one out back. Her gaze traveled over the snow, between the trees—oaks that had lost their leaves and a few evergreens—to a metal shed in the distance. Her body tensed as she stared at the structure, expecting the murderer to step out from inside the shed.

He didn't.

With the gun feeling heavy in her hand, she returned to the kitchen and set it down on the table. She slid onto a chair and pulled the laptop closer to watch the security footage. Cole, revealed by the stable's floodlights, hosed down the hay while two dogs ran around him, barking at the fire.

The next screen showed the horses, agitated but unharmed and gathered at the end of the pasture. She strained to see anyone lurking in the shadows cast by the lights attached to poles along the ranch road.

Seconds ticked by slowly, her nerves twisted into knots. The next screen popped up and a man wearing a black jacket and ski mask stepped out from behind an old truck parked on the side of the house and aimed at Zach.

She flinched. "No!"

Her scream must have reached his ears, even if faintly. Zach spun around and the bullet whizzed by, barely missing him.

The shooter ducked behind the truck. Janel lifted her hand to her head and drew in deep, settling breaths. *God, please protect Zach.*

Another camera angle flipped onto the largest section of the screen. A different masked man, also wearing all black, stood at the opposite end of the house. Zach was right; they had learned from the mistakes they made last night.

Her heart lurched as the intruder held up a gun and crept closer.

Zach needed to deal with his own shooter, who was drawing him away from the house.

Cole needed to put out a fire to save the stables.

And she needed to face a killer—all by herself.

The perpetrator reached out from the other side of an old ranch truck and discharged his weapon. Zach ducked behind Cole's parked SUV. Hearing footfalls, he inched toward the bumper in a crouched position.

A bullet fired from a different direction and shattered the window above Zach's head. He jerked away, his chest tightening with intense emotions. He had to suppress his anger and fear in order to think straight and stay alive—to keep Janel alive. Caught in a crossfire, he leaned against the tire so no one could hit him by aiming under the car.

He held his breath and listened. The familiar sound of a family pickup truck carried over a gust of wind. Straining to see the entrance to the ranch, he spotted Cole racing over the snow on horseback to prevent their father from driving into an ambush.

Zach clenched his jaw while maintaining a secure grip on his Glock.

Another engine roared, and he snuck a peek. The shooter skyrocketed over the snow, driving an ATV. He stopped about fifty feet away to collect his accomplice, a tall man wearing a similar black jacket and ski mask. A crossbow hung over his back. He'd shot the flaming arrows into the hay.

Rushing out from behind the SUV, Zach chased after them, pausing only to aim at the ATV's tire. They jolted forward and his bullet missed. Not by much. Before he could aim again, the man sitting behind the driver reached into his jacket pocket. He held up a grenade, pulled the pin and threw it at him before they took off at high speeds.

Adrenaline shot through Zach's body as he dove behind a copse of oak trees. The ground shook from the blast. Shrapnel, dirt and rock flew through the air. Seconds later, shaken but okay, he pushed to his feet. The debris had fallen short of his body by a mere six feet. Knowing better than to run after men with grenades, he headed home.

Suddenly, gunshots fired in rapid succession from the other side of the house, and a different ATV took off from that area, the driver wearing all black. A third shooter? Where did he come from? This wasn't just an attack, it was an ambush.

Zach raced across the backyard, then stopped to peer around the corner. The barrel of a gun stuck out of the guest bedroom window, firing in rapid succession toward the escaping ATV.

Janel? He did tell her to shoot at anyone who got past him.

If he said anything while outside, she might react before thinking and fire at him. Instead, he ran to the porch and unlocked the door.

"Janel!" He cautiously walked through the living room, the sound of gunshots echoing down the hall. "It's me, Zach! Don't shoot."

Silence.

"Zach?" She emerged from the door, her eyes wide and glassy. The muzzle of the revolver faced the tile floor. "It was him. I recognized the way he walked. He was coming to the house—to kill me."

"You're safe now. They're gone." He holstered his gun, then reached out for the Smith & Wesson. After taking it from her hand, he wrapped his arm around her shoulder. Then, glancing into the room, he spotted four other guns lying on the bed. "Backups?"

"I was afraid if I stopped to reload, he would run to the window and shoot me."

A smile tugged at his lips. "Good thinking. I'm proud of you." The sound of keys in the front door lock told him they were no longer alone. "That would be my dad and Cole."

Zach collected the weapons on the bed while she locked the bedroom window. He wished he hadn't left her alone. His goal was to intercept the intruder before he could get close to the house, and if they hadn't brought more men this time, he would have succeeded.

Tonight, their attackers heightened their efforts. He had to do the same.

They met up with the others in the living room.

"Are you both okay?" Cole asked.

"Terrified, but alive." Janel headed toward the kitchen. "I'm going to make more tea."

Sirens blared, and Zach shook his head. "So much for increased patrols in the area."

"I'll deal with them." Cole stepped back outside with their father.

Tired, both physically and mentally, Zach joined Janel in the kitchen. He would update his lieutenant after he made sure she was truly okay.

Janel turned on the stove beneath the kettle and then slid into a chair. "Do you think they knew most of your family had been pulled away from the ranch?"

He glanced at the charger on the counter. "Your phone wasn't on long enough for them to have used spyware to hear our conversations. They know about cameras. They turned off the one in your gallery."

"If I were them, I would strap one in the trees near the ranch. Maybe more than one."

"You're right. I would, too. They probably knew Cole and I were the only people here to look after you."

She looked taken aback. "I did a pretty good job of protecting myself."

"You were impressive. You're turning into a real cowgirl." He felt his brief smile fall. "Now, let's hope you don't have to do it again." But he knew she might—sooner rather than later.

ELEVEN

The next morning, Janel carried a cup of coffee loaded with creamer into the ranch living room for her sister while Zach sat within hearing distance at the dining room table. With Karla's many bruises, aches and pains, it was difficult to believe she only sprained her wrist in the accident.

"A thought occurred to me late last night. Maybe these guys know I have temporary amnesia. One of them could have snooped around the emergency room when I was there."

"It's a possibility." Karla straightened on the sofa and accepted the steaming cup with her one good hand.

"The rapid pace of their attacks feels desperate, but could also be part of their overall plan." Janel eased onto the ottoman across from her sister. "They might be trying to scare those memories deep into my subconscious until they can kill me."

"The doctor did say you needed to relax or you might not remember the events leading up to the concussion." Karla sipped her coffee while worry lines fanned her eyes. "This is your way of telling me you still plan to take another field trip, isn't it?"

"It's more important than ever." She reached out to touch her sister's knee. "My memories are fragile, but vital to ending this nightmare."

"Then I'm going with you and Zach."

"Absolutely not. You need to recover from the crash. And I'm not letting you change my mind this time."

Zach joined them from the dining room. "The purpose of the trip is to jog Janel's memory. That isn't going to happen if she's worried about you."

Karla finally agreed. "Please be careful. Regardless of whether these guys are trying to scare you, they are determined to fight it out rather than leave the state. There's something powerful keeping them here."

"And they have resources. We went from one assailant to two, and now three." Janel chose not to mention the grenade; Karla wouldn't let her out the door if she knew. "But we have God on our side. How else would we keep surviving hit after hit?"

Karla, not a believer, nodded slightly. "Maybe you're right."

Janel's mood lightened. Her sister might come around yet.

Minutes later, Zach drove toward the ranch's

front gate in the sheriff's vehicle while she sat next to him, scanning their surroundings for the masked men. The only movements came from the horses grazing in the pasture. The peaceful scene reminded her there were people in this world who went about their days without the worry of being shot.

If only she could turn back time and choose a different path on the day of the burglary. But she couldn't. And now she was more determined than ever to uncover the truth. Why did she follow the killer instead of going back to work after her meeting at the bank? Everything in her said she didn't know the dark-haired man personally. Did that mean she didn't know him at all?

Todd... Did he hire these guys to commit the burglary at her request? At the time, she'd given up hope God had a long-term plan for her and was desperate to keep her mother's paintings. This scenario would explain why her ex thought they had a chance of reconciling. It would also explain why he left the state.

Zach turned onto the road that would take them through Sedona and glanced at her. Concern filled his eyes. "You okay?"

She nodded, despite feeling nauseated by her thoughts. Dark, threatening clouds loomed ahead, a mirror reflection of her mood. "Zach, thank you for taking me up the mountain. I know you don't like leaving the ranch."

"That was before."

"Before?" She raised her brows at his gruff tone.

"Before we met Frank Hyde yesterday." Zach's jaw tightened as he gripped the steering wheel with both hands. "I've met men like him before. I have no doubt this insurance investigator will bend the facts to make you look guilty. We need to do everything we can to mount your defense."

"I hope returning to the spot where the murderer climbed into the landscaping truck with the redhead will help me remember more."

Stealing a glance toward Zach, she wished her life was different. That she wasn't attracting danger, and she felt emotionally strong enough to make wise decisions. She believed he was a good man. He acted like one. But was he the man for her...one day far in the future? If she were found innocent of the burglary? She didn't know for sure.

Raindrops dotted the car as they drove through Sedona. Zach waited until they covered the windshield to flip on the wiper. "I hope the sky is clear going up the mountain."

"Weather shouldn't be a problem." She replayed the recently recalled memory. "I stayed in the car that morning, so there's no need to get out and retrace my footsteps. And who knows? Maybe we'll find his silver sedan parked on the side of the road."

"Probably not, but like you said, who knows?"

Fifteen minutes later, they left Sedona and drove the two-lane road through Oak Creek Canyon. Winter hikers rushed over the snow to their vehicles as sprinkles turned into a downpour. One car after another passed them on their way out of the scenic area.

Red rocks and oak trees soon gave way to pine trees and switchbacks as they climbed the mountain. The narrow roads made her nervous, especially in construction areas like this one. The drop-off on their right kept Zach driving close to the center line. With the storm sending most people indoors, the traffic thinned and then became almost nonexistent.

Lightning lit up the sky. Through the rain-streaked window, she spotted the blue helicopter she'd seen right before Karla's car accident. A man wearing a black ski mask held a rifle outside the door. He aimed directly at them.

Her eyes widened.

"Shooter!" She heard a pop and felt a sudden jerk.

"He hit our tire!" The sheriff's vehicle swerved. Zach slammed on the brakes while gripping the steering wheel, trying to regain control, but the front end drove out over the side of the mountain, pushing on the orange netting meant to warn drivers to stay on the road.

The car stopped moving. The undercarriage

of the car rested on the edge of a cliff, but they weren't tipping—yet. Movement of any kind might send them over. She held her breath, not ready to put her faith in an orange safety net that might not hold their weight. Instead, she prayed.

A vehicle rounded the winding road farther up the mountain, and the *wyump, wyump* of the helicopter's whirling blades faded as they flew away.

"What do we do now?" Pressing her back against her seat, she froze in place. All she could hear was her heartbeat, despite the rain pelting the windows.

Zach looked around, his expression grim. "We can't stay here."

"I vote we do. I'm scared." Her breathing grew ragged, her chest felt heavy and her head throbbed.

"The shooter will most likely come back to see the damage they caused. If we're alive—"

"We won't be for long. I get the picture." She groaned. "And I thought driving off a cliff into a creek filled with raging water was bad."

"You can do this." He reached his hand out to cover hers. "We have to, but slowly."

The warmth of his touch reminded her she wasn't alone. Together, they were stronger. "What happens if we open the doors—slowly—and the car tips over?"

"Jump out. Immediately." His wide eyes and tone demanded she take him seriously. "Ready?"

She barely nodded, still afraid to move but trying to look on the bright side. They had overcome so much already. How hard could this be?

Zach reached for his handle. "Unlock your door." When she paused, he whispered, "Janel, you need to unlock your door."

Biting her lip, she clicked the power button. "Do we open the doors on three?"

"Sounds good. One."

Horrified by what might happen, she screamed, "Wait!"

"Two. Three."

Having no choice, she pulled the handle and pushed against her door when he did. The sky rained on the arm of her coat.

The car creaked beneath them.

Her breath hitched.

Peering down, she eyed the cliff's edge below her seat. She blinked hard, diverting her gaze from where she might fall. Directly in front of her was maybe a four-inch width of solid ground for her to take her first step. Maybe she should crawl out.

The car slid forward another inch.

Her entire body shook.

"Jump!"

His loud, commanding voice propelled her forward. She fell onto her hands, with one knee landing on solid ground covered with patches of frigid melting snow while the other hugged the side of the cliff. Rain, turning to hail, pelted her back.

Zach rushed around the back end. "Are you okay?" He pulled her to her feet as water dripped down their faces.

A sports car, driving down the switchbacks, approached quickly. Zach tried to wave the driver down, but he ignored them and increased his speed, his front tires hitting a huge puddle right next to their car.

Janel instinctively took a step back as the water and slush splashed, drenching them. She lost her balance and screamed as she slipped beneath the orange netting and fell over the side of the mountain. Air whooshed out of her lungs.

She reached for a crevice but missed. Then her fingers skimmed a thick tree root, and she immediately grabbed hold of the hard rope-like feature that looped out and back into the mountainside.

The freezing hail struck her face as thunder filled her ears. Looking up, she found Zach reaching out to her.

With feet dangling below her, she tried to force her hand to let go of the root, but sheer terror controlled her body. Her fingers ached from holding on so tightly. Logic told her she couldn't stay there; she'd grow tired and fall to her death. But she couldn't move, either. Tears clouded her eyes and slid down her cheeks, dropping into thin air. Who knew where they would eventually land?

Was she really going to die—here—after everything she fought against already?

"Janel, grab my hand." He leaned out farther. "You can do this. Trust me."

A gust of wind made her shiver as the torrential rains threatened her ability to hold on. She prayed for help. "God, please don't let me fall."

Fear squeezed Zach's heart as he peered down at Janel. She hung from a tree root on the side of the mountain that had been carved out to keep boulders from falling on the road far below. If she let go, it would be a straight sixty-foot drop onto hard ground. He could not lose her, especially like this.

"Janel, look at me." Stretched out over the muddy ground, with the rain beating down on them, he continued to reach for her. Their hands were roughly two feet apart, and he couldn't move any closer without risking both their lives.

She tried, but rainwater hit her eyes, forcing her to blink and turn away. "I can't." Her entire body shook, then she made the mistake of looking down and began hyperventilating. "I don't want to die," she pleaded.

"I won't let you." He could hear the desperation in his voice. "Please, take my hand."

"I'm afraid to let go."

"You have no choice." He had to make her try. A memory of them talking at church flashed through his mind. "Janel, close your eyes and ask God for help."

"I already did." One hand slipped off the root. She gasped and kicked her boots wildly in the air as she grabbed hold again.

Horror struck him. "Pray for strength!"

"God, please save me!" she screamed and shot one hand up into the air.

Zach grabbed her wrist and pulled her up and over the side. Together, they fell into the mud. He didn't care; she was safe in his arms. Overwhelmed with emotion, a single tear slid down the side of his face. *Thank You, God. Thank You.*

Sobs racked her body as he held her close, patting the back of her coat.

After the worst was over, he helped her up and walked her away from the edge of the mountain. "We need to get away from here before they come back."

A frigid wind swept over them, and she shuddered. "You saved my life—again."

Guilt nudged at him. "We wouldn't have been here if it weren't for me."

"Don't say that. We both agreed it's important for me to remember why I followed the murderer, and if I saw his face."

"You're right." He had to stop being so hard on himself. Only in a perfect world could she lie low until the shooters were caught. Their situation grew worse by the minute, and he needed her help.

Zach removed his cell phone from his pocket, hoping to call for a tow truck and a ride home. "I can't get a bar. The mountain and rain are interfering with the signal."

"Then we walk." She glanced up at the dark clouds, then wiped the water from her face. "Like you said, we don't want to wait here for that helicopter to come back."

After tightening his coat's hood around his face, he reached for her hand, not wanting to risk anything else happening to her. If he kept her close, he could pull her out of danger—in time, he hoped. At least the rain would keep most cars off the road, reducing the likelihood of getting hit since there wasn't much of a dirt shoulder to walk on. The rainwater would also wash away the mud covering them.

Lightning lit up the sky and thunder roared as they strode down the mountain toward a cabin his friend Joe owned, about five miles away.

He looked forward to reaching shelter. Careless drivers and shooters weren't the only dangers they had to look out for. There were still areas on the mountain where rain could dislodge huge rocks, sending them down on top of them.

Their eagerness to reach a safe and dry location kept their pace swift and the conversation to a minimum.

After walking for almost an hour, Janel sighed. "Are we there yet?"

He squeezed her hand. "Almost."

Fifteen minutes later, he led her up the muddy, unpaved driveway to a log cabin. The blinds were closed in the windows, the porch light was on during the day, and the fact Joe traveled for a living all pointed to his friend being out of town.

When no one answered his knock, Zach reached around a bush for the fake rock that held the spare front door key. "Joe said I had an open invitation."

"How long have you been friends?"

"Twenty years." He unlocked the door and entered first. A quick look around confirmed his suspicions—Joe's razor, toothbrush and comb were missing from the medicine cabinet. "He's not here. I'll leave him a note."

"What about your phone? Can you get a signal?"

Zach checked. "Three bars." His first call was to Cole. The second to his lieutenant, and he emphasized the sheriff's vehicle hadn't gone over the edge of the mountain. His third call was to Lily, who knew the way to the cabin. "We're going to need a ride back to the ranch once the rain lets up."

"I'll text you before I leave." Lily ended with, "Try not to get shot at while you wait."

"That's the plan."

Zach caught sight of Janel hanging her wet coat over the back of a kitchen chair, before grabbing a throw blanket from a recliner and wrapping it around her shoulders. She was beautiful, even with her hair soaked and hugging her face. When her gaze locked on his, he blurted, "I'll light a fire."

"That would be wonderful." She hugged the blanket close before joining him at the stone fireplace.

Once the flames crackled, they sat on the hearth, soaking up the warmth. When she shuddered, he ran his hands along her arms, trying to force the cold away. "Is that better?"

She nodded, looking up at him. "Thank you for telling me to pray when I was hanging from that tree root. I hadn't felt God's presence in a long time, but he was there on the side of that mountain. In that second, I knew without a doubt that I would be safe. He wouldn't let me fall. That's why I didn't hesitate that last time to reach for you."

"I was terrified that I might lose you." Remembering those feelings lowered his guard, and the reasons they couldn't be together didn't seem so important.

"Lose me?" Her soft, questioning voice pushed any remaining reservations aside.

He stroked her soft jaw. "I feel strongly about you. I know we've been friends for years, but I'm hoping that maybe one day we could be more."

With gazes locked, she leaned closer, and he kissed her. Tenderly at first, then more fully. This moment felt right. They belonged together. Now he held no doubts.

A house-shaking thunderbolt jerked them apart.

Then Zach heard the hum of a car engine outside.

TWELVE

Zach separated the blinds enough to look out into the storm. The hairs on his neck stood on end when a car rolled by slower than the weather called for. "There's a silver sedan outside. The windows are fogged, so I can't see the driver."

"The guy who shot the redhead drove a silver sedan before he switched to the landscaping truck."

"It's gone now." Zach placed his hand on the handle of his holstered gun. "I won't let him come anywhere near you."

"I know." The worry etched into her face remained, despite his reassurances. As if needing to see for herself, she peeked out through the window. "If it's the murderer, he might drive up the mountain and discover we left the car behind."

"He might not turn around and search for us," Zach spoke without taking his attention away from the window. The heavy clouds, rain-soaked trees and deserted road gave off an eerie vibe.

"That might be too much to hope for." She

retreated to the dining room table and glanced about. "Would your friend mind if I made coffee?"

"Not at all." He told her where to find a canister of ground coffee and filters.

She took over from there, which gave him time to think about the kiss they'd shared and about how he'd become lost in the moment. He'd wanted to tell her how much she meant to him, and how he wanted to become a couple. But he couldn't. Not yet.

While listening to the coffee drip into the pot, he wondered about Janel's relationship with Todd. They'd dated for years. Were they truly in love? If so, he had to bow out and give her time to recover emotionally from their split…or go back to the man, if that's what she wanted.

But what if she and Todd weren't in love? Was there room for him now? Perhaps her grief over her mother's illness and later passing away were too strong for her to see the reality of the relationship back then. If so, how could she be better off now? The stress over her concussion, memory loss, potentially losing her gallery, her mother's missing painting and running for her life would be too much for anyone to handle.

He and Janel needed to talk about their kiss. Eventually. They were too on edge to have that conversation right now. Minutes later, she carried a cup of coffee for him to the window, where they could see the rain was letting up.

His phone dinged with an incoming text. "It's Lily. She's a mile away." He swallowed several gulps before handing the cup back. "I'll deal with the fireplace."

"I'll clean up the kitchen."

They had just finished when he heard the hum of an engine and car tires crunching gravel. Zach flipped off the inside lights, then made sure it was safe to exit before locking up and leading her to his mother's Cadillac. His sister sat behind the wheel.

They secured their seat belts while Lily announced unsettling news. "Cole says I need to take you both to Janel's house. Karla is already there."

"She's still recovering from her crash." Confusion registered in Janel's expression when she turned to Zach. "Do you know what's going on?"

"No, but I don't like it at all." He clenched his jaw. None of this felt right.

Sitting in the back seat, Zach squeezed Janel's hand several times on the way. She could only muster a partial smile in return. He remembered her telling him about the house she and Karla had inherited and how it felt empty without their mother, especially with her sister working in Scottsdale.

Looking out the windows, he studied their surroundings, keeping an eye out for any shooters. At least the rain had stopped, and the storm clouds were drifting away. That was one thing in their favor.

Driving down her block, he counted five vehicles parked on the curb, two marked Sheriff and one belonging to Cole. The front door opened, and Karla, cradling her braced wrist, marched across the grassy lawn toward them.

"Thanks, Lily," Zach said. "We'll catch a ride back with Cole."

"Anytime. My taxi service is always available." In a more serious tone, Lily added, "I'll pray things go well for you here."

The second the vehicle stopped, they pushed open their doors and Janel rushed to her sister. "What's going on?"

"They have a search warrant." A mask of disgust marred Karla's features.

"Who has a warrant?" Agitated, Janel ran her hand through her damp hair. "There's nothing here worth this kind of effort."

"Zach's lieutenant, his deputies, a Scottsdale detective and that slimy insurance investigator, Frank Hyde." Karla's voice heightened as she rattled off each person. "They think Mom's missing painting is here."

"What?" Janel took two steps forward, then stopped and rubbed the chill from her arms. Their clothing was still damp from their walk down the mountain in the rain. She should change while they were here.

"Hurry," Karla urged. "I don't want Hyde wandering around the house unsupervised."

Zach, with his long stride, beat them to the door while Lily drove away.

Once inside, Cole hurried over. He wasted no time filling them in. "When your lieutenant couldn't reach you, he called me. The guy with the mustache standing next to the dining room table is Detective Everly from Scottsdale. He says he arrested a fence who claimed he's been buying stolen art from Karla for the past year."

"No." Janel shook her head vehemently. "That's a lie."

Her sister's eyes narrowed. "He's lying."

Zach nodded his understanding, although he wasn't ready to make any declarations of innocence yet. He barely knew Karla.

A deputy finished searching the coat closet, and Zach reached inside. "Why search here?" he asked Cole while handing Janel a heavy sweater. "Karla lives in Scottsdale."

Janel hung her damp coat from the closet doorknob. Shrugging into the dry sweater, she stared at a deputy in the living room. He had removed seat cushions from the sofa, and it must have felt like he was tearing her home apart. There was nothing Zach could do about it. He felt helpless.

"The news gets worse," Cole said, jerking

Zach's attention back to the conversation. "The fence claimed Janel called him the morning of the burglary, wanting to sell him four bronze statues."

Her eyes grew wide. "I don't know any fences."

Frank Hyde stepped out of the hallway. The smug look he wore said he'd overheard them. "The fence, Axel, was arrested before your scheduled meeting. Otherwise, he would have been caught with the goods."

"I never set up a meeting." Janel glared at Hyde.

Karla fisted her hands and stepped toward him. Zach blocked her path forward. This wasn't the time for a brawl.

"We found something." Voices drifted in from the opened sliding glass back door.

"The deputies couldn't have found anything connected to the burglary," Janel insisted. "It's not possible." She followed Zach out her back door. The snow around the pavers had turned to slush, so she watched her step on the way to the small art studio. Her mother had built it in the yard after they moved to this community near Sedona.

The lieutenant reached the studio door before them. "Wait here," he instructed. "Detectives, join me inside."

Janel wanted to protest as Cole and the Scottsdale detective were granted access, but not her. This was her home. Karla's, too, if she ever moved here. And their mother's painting space was like a memorial. The two of them had left it untouched, other than sweeping the floor and dusting. Whenever they missed her more than usual, they sat inside and reminisced. The thought that strangers had rifled through every drawer and cupboard made her stomach churn.

A deputy stood guard at the door, blocking the entrance, while Frank Hyde, the independent investigator hired by the insurance company, carried his leather notebook and paced the patio. He wore the same black T-shirt and gray suit he had on the previous evening. Karla glared at him, but he didn't seem to notice.

Zach leaned close to Janel and whispered, "What's in there?"

"My mother's art supplies. And the painting she was working on when she passed away. A rainbow above Cathedral Rock." Growing emotions, caught in her throat, threatened to choke her. She might need a lawyer, but asking for one could make her appear guilty.

"When was the last time you were in there?" Zach placed his hand on her arm, his expression sympathetic.

"Two weeks ago, and everything looked untouched. I don't understand what they think they've found."

After several long minutes, the lieutenant called them inside. The aroma of linseed oil wafted through the room. The deputies must have opened the one remaining bottle. She was glad to see they had put away anything they had searched through.

Fully inside the room, her boot heels clicked on the tile floor as she walked toward the easel that was turned in a different direction. Looking down, she found her mother's unfinished painting resting against the wooden easel leg. Her instinct was to snatch it up off the floor, but Cole stopped her.

"Don't touch anything," he instructed. "We have to check for fingerprints."

Annoyed that her mother's final work would get dirty on the floor, Janel stepped around to the front of the easel to see what was on display instead of the other painting. She blinked, then stared in disbelief at the sweeping swirls of red and orange. *Sun Setting on Rocks.* The missing painting. Her mother's legacy was all accounted for now.

Relief washed over her. "How did it get here?"

Instead of answering her question, Cole asked one of his own. "Are you positive it's your mother's work?"

"*I* am, and it was *planted* here." Karla pointed to Frank Hyde. "You refuse to see that because you want me to go to jail. You're after my job. It's common knowledge at the insurance company. How many times have you dropped hints around my coworkers? Six? Seven? I've got news for you—they will never hire you full-time. They don't like your methods."

Hyde snapped pictures of the painting with his phone, then smiled at her. "They'll like my methods now. And I want you to go to *prison*, not just jail, because you are behind the string of burglaries you supposedly couldn't solve. And now your sister is in on the act. She set up the burglary at her own gallery, and I'm going to prove it."

"The art has been retrieved, so your job here is done." Zach addressed his next comment to the Scottsdale detective. "I don't understand why the judge signed a warrant to search a house in my county. No offense, but this isn't your jurisdiction."

"No offense taken." The Scottsdale detective, a quiet man with brown curly hair, placed his hand on his hip near the badge attached to his waist. "The fence claiming he bought art stolen from Karla Newman is in my jurisdiction, and her name is on the deed to this house, along with her sister's. Plus, we had an anonymous tip."

Zach lifted his brow. "What tip?"

Hyde lifted his finger, indicating he wanted to talk. "I received a voicemail message saying we could find stolen artwork here."

"That's convenient," Janel murmured, feeling like a spider caught in a web of deceit. Her sister was right; someone planted the painting here. There was no other reasonable explanation, and if these men didn't see that, she and Karla were in a world of hurt.

Anger flashed across Karla's face as she spoke to the detective. "I'm the one who put you on to the fence's trail. *I found* the informant who said Axel was buying the stolen art." Not missing a beat, she turned her ire on Hyde. "Did you ever consider the possibility they broke into my sister's gallery to keep me off the case because I was getting too close?"

"You make a valid point." The Scottsdale detective paused momentarily, as if ruminating over the facts. "I don't know what's going on here. The lieutenant says someone has tried to kill both you and your sister. And now this." He gestured to the painting. "If I were you, I would hire a bodyguard and an excellent lawyer."

"What?" Hyde shook his head. "You're not going to let them walk, are you?"

Annoyance flickered across the detective's stoic features. "This painting is evidence in Detective Walker's Sedona case, not mine. Nothing else was found here. I'm heading back to Scottsdale. Don't call me again unless you personally see proof related to *my* case."

Frustrated, Hyde stormed out of the studio.

Relieved, Janel retreated to her yard. Zach followed her, but then Cole called him back inside.

"I'll wait for you on the patio," she promised. Surely, she'd be safe with so many law enforcement officers on her property. Seconds later, she removed the wet covers from two chairs and sank into thick cushions. Her sister claimed the chair beside her.

Karla snarled. "Hyde always gets on my last nerve."

When Janel studied the fierce expression on her sister's face, she suddenly felt ill. A memory flickered through her mind. The morning of the burglary. In Sedona. Outside of a coffee shop. Karla, looking as angry as she did now, drew back her hand to slap a dark-haired man. He caught her wrist before she could follow through with the motion.

Janel had witnessed this while seated in her car at a traffic light. After leaving the bank, she headed back to work. Karla mentioned that morning that she was coming to town because of the burglary. She must have stopped for coffee and run into this man.

A flood of memories returned, and Janel's pulse raced. Breathing proved difficult as she remembered watching the man turn around. He wore mirror-lensed sunglasses and a black jacket with a hood hanging over his back. The murderer. Nausea struck her, and she felt lightheaded.

Karla, in real time, stood in front of her, waving her hands to capture her attention. Janel closed her eyes, not wanting her returning memories to slip away. *Why did I follow him?*

Suddenly, she pictured this man at her gallery last week. He'd spent at least twenty minutes studying her most expensive pieces, including her mother's paintings that were not for sale. He checked his cell phone between admiring one item after another but didn't buy anything. Had he been casing her gallery?

Her thoughts traveled back to the café parking lot. If asked why she wanted to slap him, Karla would have said it was nothing to worry about. So, wanting answers, Janel decided to follow the man. If he had been casing her gallery and stole from her, perhaps she'd find a clue leading to her mother's paintings.

Once Karla and the man climbed into their own vehicles and departed, Janel made sure she stayed at least two car lengths behind the dark-haired man.

After leaving Sedona and driving up the switchbacks, he left his silver sedan on the shoulder of the forest road to climb into the landscaping truck. That led to the two men parking in front of the white Victorian house. The dark-haired man walked toward the casita where her stolen art was hidden. The redheaded man attempted a double cross but was shot and killed. Horrified, Janel had gasped. The murderer spotted her and the race for her life began.

Then Zach saved her.

Janel blinked rapidly as her mind came out

of her daze. A rush of emotions swept over her. She pressed her fingers against her forehead and closed her eyes.

Karla grabbed Janel's shoulders. "Talk to me. What's wrong?"

"I remember *everything.*"

"That's great!"

Confused, she looked up at her sister, ready to read her reactions to the truth. "You haven't been up front with me."

"What are you talking about?" Deep lines creased Karla's forehead.

"You know the man who chased me through the forest. You tried to slap him outside of a coffee shop. *I saw you.*" Janel now understood why her memories had eluded her. They were too painful to face. Her sister was somehow connected to a murderer.

Karla quietly stared at the ground.

Janel pressed on. "He knew which car was yours when he planted the bomb because he saw you driving it. Why did he try to blow you up? I understand why he shot at me. I saw him kill the redhead. Did you see him kill someone?"

"No. I always turn my car on with the fob, and he knows that. Maybe he was trying to scare you into keeping quiet." Karla glanced toward the sheriff's deputies on the other side of the yard. "I swear I didn't know he was the man trying to kill you until you connected all the pieces just now."

Janel grabbed her sister's arm. "What's his name?"

"Shh. You'll attract attention." Karla jerked free of her grip and then leaned closer. "This is worse than you think. If Hyde persuades a district attorney to arrest either of us for the string of thefts he and his brothers committed, the charges will include accessory to murder."

Hyde could have them arrested for murder? Her mind refused to accept the possibility. She shook her head. "This isn't happening."

Karla pushed out of the chair. "I'll fix this."

Wanting answers, she followed her sister inside the house. "What do you mean by 'fix this'?"

"Exactly what I said." With the law enforcement officers all outside, Karla removed their mother's car keys from a kitchen drawer. "The next time you see me, you won't have to worry about anyone trying to frame us, and Zach can make his arrests. Until then, I need you to keep this between the two of us. If anyone stops me, I can't prove our innocence."

"What did you get yourself mixed up in?" Stunned, Janel stood there, watching her sister exit out the garage door. Could Karla really solve their problems, or was this the beginning of a horrible end for them both?

THIRTEEN

Zach had wanted to believe from day one that Janel was innocent, and recent events only confirmed his gut feeling. She was too smart to display a stolen painting on an easel. Plus, she never would have disrespected her mother's unfinished work by leaving the canvas on the studio floor.

He told Cole as much during their conversation in Janel's living room while she'd gone to change into dry clothes. "What do we do now?"

Cole crossed his hands over his chest. "For starters, we can check the gallery's security technician off our list of suspects. He's worked for the company for fifteen years. Respected. No outstanding debts. No obvious suspicious spending."

"Sounds clean to me."

"Another thing," Cole continued. "Remember the casita where we found the other paintings?"

Zach nodded. "The one where the security camera had been turned off."

"The wires were cut. But the cameras attached to the house were still working."

"They must have used jammers to get inside both the casita and the gallery, just like the string of burglaries Karla was investigating."

"My thoughts exactly," Cole shared. "They needed to disable the camera inside the casita because the stolen art was out in the open. The owner could have gone online to check on his property while he was in Florida."

"So, we're dealing with intelligent burglars, who are *not* computer hackers, but did gain access to Janel's security code." Zach rubbed his chin with the pad of his thumb, trying to think of any other leads they may have forgotten to pursue. "Did you ever get a hold of the former boyfriend?"

"No answer. I left Todd a message to call me."

"He could be busy at his friend's wedding." Zach removed his cowboy hat and ran his hand through his hair. He was still a disheveled mess from walking in the rain and hail.

Leaning to the side, Cole glanced down the hall as if making sure Janel wasn't headed their way before he spoke. "What about Karla? She seemed eager to take off. Do you think she could be involved?"

For Janel's sake, Zach hoped not. "It wouldn't make sense for Karla to give information about the fence to the Scottsdale detective if she were the one selling him the stolen art."

"Unless she suspected the detective was already hot on his trail, and she wanted to make sure no one believed the fence if he named her."

Zach blew out a long breath. "I wish you hadn't said that."

"Why?"

"If Karla is involved in these burglaries, including the Sedona gallery, Janel will never get over it. It's her twin we're talking about."

Footsteps clicking on the tile floor ended their conversation. Seconds later, Janel entered the living room, carrying a garment bag. "I figured I'd better bring more clothes back to the ranch. I hope you don't mind."

"Not at all. It's a good idea." Zach strode over and collected the bag from her. "Cole's giving us a lift."

She sent his brother a tenuous smile. "This seems to be a repeating pattern. We get shot at and you drive us to the ranch."

"A pattern I hope to break soon by making an arrest." Cole waved them toward the front door.

Worry lines creased her face.

"You all right?" Zach asked, knowing no one could truly be "all right" when they've endured so much in such a short time.

She nodded, then silently walked to the front door and locked it after they were all outside.

The quiet in Cole's SUV was deafening. No one felt like talking, and if they did, they received one-word answers. They were all tired. It had been a long, overwhelming day.

Zach had so many questions to ask Janel, but he wanted to wait until they were alone. Driving through Sedona, the hum of the engine had almost lulled him to sleep in the passenger seat when he heard the whirr of helicopter blades.

"Is that the shooter? Please tell me it's not him," Janel called out from the back, panic infused in every word.

They peered through the vehicle's windows, trying to spot the helicopter. Cole had to slow down when the light up ahead turned red. They were boxed in by the heavy traffic.

"It's close." Zach rolled down his window to get a better look. Sure enough, a blue helicopter hovered high above them. "It looks like the same one."

Janel leaned closer to the front seat. "He won't shoot with this many witnesses, will he?"

"I want to say no," Zach answered. "But these men are desperate and anything but predictable. Although…" Remembering where they were, he had an idea. "Cole, take us to the police station. Let's see how daring these guys really are."

"You got it." Cole flipped on the siren and radioed the station to alert them to a potential danger.

The helicopter flew off. Zach tried to find identifying marks, but it was too far away. He called his lieutenant, who promised to get eyes in the sky.

The light turned green and the cars ahead of them moved out of the way. Cole sped to the police station, where several officers stood out front, waiting for them.

When the SUV parked at the front entrance, Zach told Janel to wait for him to get out first. When no one shot at him, he opened her door. "Walk quickly inside, then stay away from the windows."

"I'm so tired of being shot at." She unbuckled her seat belt and bolted toward the doors.

"Me, too." He stayed close, his body shielding hers.

"This way." Cole led them to his office, a cubicle in a large room. On his desk was a picture of his wife, Sierra. She had once been chased by a bomber. This was a reminder that good triumphs over evil when God is on your side. Sometimes it took longer to see the results, but Zach always saw the positive outcome in the end.

After Cole left them alone, Zach found another chair and pulled it into the cubicle to sit next to Janel. "This will be over before you know it."

"And then what?" Her eyes pleaded for an answer.

He wanted to make her promises, but he knew he couldn't. "I pray God will put these men behind bars, and soon."

Janel sat silently, rubbing her hands over her crossed arms.

Impatient for an update, Zach checked the window several times. He neither saw nor heard the helicopter. It was long gone.

Every time he sat, he studied Janel, finding her both strong and fragile. She would do what was needed to stay alive, even fire a gun, but she wore her heart on her sleeve. The thought reminded him of their kiss. "Janel…"

"There's something you need to know," she stated, stopping him from exploring where they stood romantically. "When I was sitting on my porch and you were in the art studio, a memory came back to me. I did see the dark-haired man's face, just like you thought. I don't know him, but I doubt Frank Hyde can be convinced of that. He thinks I'm guilty."

"You remember his face, and you didn't tell me?" Zach shook his head in disbelief.

She reached for the barely visible bump on her head. "It just came back to me at the house. So much happened there, and this is the first time we've been alone."

"You could have told Cole and me after everyone left."

"I wasn't ready," she snapped. "I'm sorry. Please forgive me for raising my voice. I'm trying to sort all of this out and needed time."

"I understand." At least, he thought he did. "Did you remember anything else?"

"He was in the gallery last week. I think he was casing the place. He had an eye for valuable art with resell potential. I thought he was interested in purchasing a piece as an investment, but he left without buying anything."

"Is that why you followed him? Because you thought he might be one of the burglars?"

"Yeah." Her gaze lowered to the industrial carpet. "I know it was foolish, but I was hoping he would lead me to my mother's paintings."

Before he could ask another question, Cole stepped inside the door. "False alarm. It turns out the helicopter is owned by a real estate developer. The pilot was carrying a photographer hired to take aerial shots of a property for sale, and the local tourist sites."

Zach glanced up at his brother. "Did the pilot say why he took off so fast?"

"Police sirens." Cole pointed to himself. "My siren. He thought it best to get out of the way in case there was trouble."

"Smart," Janel concluded before her gaze traveled between the brothers. "Cole, I remembered what the murderer looks like."

"That's great! This is the breakthrough we needed." He rushed behind his desk. "Since I have you here, do you mind looking at mug shots of men arrested for burglary in Arizona?"

"I guess not," she said, but the worry lines on her face said something different.

Zach reached over and squeezed her hand. After everything she'd been through, he couldn't blame her for not looking forward to studying photographs of men with criminal histories, especially when the right one might take her emotionally back to the forest when she was running for her life.

The next morning, Janel entered the bedroom where Karla usually slept, hoping she had returned to the ranch during the early morning hours. There had been no sign of her the previous night.

Janel sat on the blue and white quilt covering the perfectly made queen-size bed and tried to reach Karla again. When the call went to voicemail, she hung up. She'd already left ten messages. How many times do you need to tell someone to call you?

Dread threatened to invade Janel's thoughts, but she wasn't ready to give up hope that her sister had safely returned to the ranch.

She checked the living room, dining room and then the kitchen before finally accepting the fact Karla was still out there somewhere. Doing what? Why did her sister think she could fix this? And how?

"Good morning." Zach stepped into the kitchen,

his boots clicking on the tile floor. The woodsy scent of his cologne wafted through the air.

"I'm not sure it is a good morning." Janel sat at the kitchen table and clasped her hands together. "I didn't recognize anyone in those mug shots. All we know about the gallery burglar is he's willing to kill, has dangerous accomplices and could have run into my sister last night."

Zach prepared two mugs of coffee and joined her. "Do you have any idea where she went?"

"I wish I did." She accepted the coffee he offered and tried to draw comfort from its warmth before placing the mug down on the table. "Karla was so angry at Hyde yesterday. He's going after us, and she's determined to stop him."

Guilt ate at Janel for telling Zach a partial truth, but revealing that Karla knew the identity of the murderer and didn't tell anyone would make her sister look complicit in his crimes. And Janel couldn't stab her twin in the back like that.

Besides, Karla needed secrecy in order to prove their innocence. She told her so.

But how could Janel enter a romantic relationship with Zach if she wasn't completely honest with him?

She couldn't. Staring down at the coffee threatening to turn cold in her mug, Janel felt a new hole growing in her heart.

Zach drank his coffee, unaware of the emo-

tional quandary she faced. "How does Karla plan
to stop Hyde?"

"By uncovering the truth."

"That's what we want, too." Zach reached
across the table to touch her hand, but she abruptly
pulled it back onto her lap. He blinked hard before confusion altered his expression. Her reaction was a far cry from the kiss they had shared
in the cabin.

"I could be in a jail cell by the end of the week,"
she said, offering some sort of explanation.

"I won't let that happen."

"No matter how hard we try, there are some
things we can't control—even when we pray.
Take my gallery, for example."

"Give it time." He leaned closer. "You prayed
you'd find your mother's paintings, and you did.
They may be in police custody for a while, but
you'll get them back."

"Or the bank will. Have you forgotten I put
them up for collateral to get my loan? My gallery
is closed, and mail orders won't keep us afloat
for long. I'll have to work for someone else while
I spend the rest of my life trying to find those
paintings and hoping I can buy them back. One
piece at a time." Her heart ached. "To make matters worse, the murderer or one of his accomplices might mistake Karla for me. My sister is
risking her life, trying to prove we're innocent.
How much can go wrong all at once?"

"You're right. The future looks bleak right now, but that's when we need to rely on our faith the most." He pulled the laptop closer. "Let's help your sister find the truth."

"How? I already looked at mug shots." Curious, she watched while sipping her coffee again.

"You said the murderer came into your gallery before the burglary. He might still be on your security footage."

Hope lit anew. When Zach turned the laptop toward her, Janel entered the URL address. While waiting for the website to load, she tried to recall the man's face. Closing her eyes, she replayed the scene where she first saw him—with her sister—in the coffee shop parking lot.

Karla had tried to slap him. He grabbed her wrist to stop her.

They argued. Karla pulled her hand back.

The man turned to leave, and Janel saw his face. Oval shaped. Clean-cut. Grecian nose. Piercing, angry eyes.

She quickly logged into her account. Scanning the page, she found the link that would show the camera footage for the day she believed he was casing her gallery. "Here we go."

Zach rounded the table to sit beside her. "What time was he there?"

"About two o'clock." She fast-forwarded the video, then slowed its progression. The picture suddenly distorted and turned black. "No…"

"One of his buddies must have jammed the camera." Zach shook his head. "If only… A picture would have gone a long way in identifying him."

Janel slumped in her chair. Suddenly, she remembered another time she saw the murderer, although briefly.

Her eyes widened. "I passed him on a sidewalk." Reenergized, she sat up straight and clicked out of the website. "I was about to enter a gala celebrating the opening of a Scottsdale gallery when he exited through the double doors. We don't know each other, so I forgot about it until now." She grinned. "The gala had an official photographer."

Zach's eyes lit up as he watched her work. "Maybe we'll catch a break after all."

She searched online for the gallery name, then scrolled through a multitude of photos.

Five minutes later, a picture and adjoining caption ignited genuine excitement. She pointed at the dark-haired man, who stood next to a museum curator and a wealthy art collector. "I found him!"

Zach pulled the screen closer to read, "Sawyer Sloan. Does the name sound familiar?"

"No, it doesn't, but then I don't leave Sedona much these days. Too busy working." She typed his name into a search engine and found a business website. "He's an art broker based in Scottsdale. He doesn't have regular office hours. You have to make an appointment to see him."

"Let's schedule one." Zach jotted down the phone number on notebook paper before calling. When no one answered, he left a message. "I'm interested in acquiring your services." He left a Biblical name but didn't mention he was a sheriff's deputy before hanging up.

"John?" she asked.

"My middle name."

"Nice. Can you check to see if he has an arrest record?"

"Sure." After a few minutes, Zach announced, "No prior arrests, but he did file a police report. His personal collection of Southwestern art was stolen a year ago."

"That is when the string of burglaries started."

Zach met her gaze. "The photographs attached to the police report were provided by the same insurance company your sister works for."

Words eluded her. Karla's specialty was art cases. This must be how she met the dark-haired murderer. Why did she try to slap him? Did she figure out he broke into Janel's gallery? If so, how? And why didn't she say anything?

While listening to Zach update his brother and lieutenant, mixed emotions assaulted Janel. A nagging fear ate at her, too. What if she just made things worse by giving law enforcement the name of the murderer? Would these masked men become more reckless with their attempts to kill her if law enforcement zeroed in on them? If so, more people would die.

FOURTEEN

An hour later, Zach continued to investigate with Janel's help. She'd fired off emails to the event coordinator in charge of invitations for the gala, and to the two men photographed with Sawyer Sloan, asking what they knew about him. She sat across from him, waiting for their replies.

Meanwhile, Zach discovered that Sawyer, who was an art broker, had two unemployed brothers living in Casa Grande, near Tucson. Oscar, nick-named Oz, did time for burglary. Mostly video game stores. Larry, who owned a motorcycle, served in the military during his early twenties, which meant he had weapons training. He was involved in a bar fight two years ago, but no one pressed charges, even though the other guy left with a broken arm.

Zach's best guess was Sawyer selected the items to steal. Oz coordinated the burglaries. And Larry led the attacks. It made sense. What he didn't know was how they got Janel's alarm code. He pictured the gallery in his mind. The front was all glass, so the alarm panel hung on an adjacent wall. One of these men could have sat in a car with binoculars and watched Janel or Charlene enter the code.

There were other pressing questions Zach wanted answered. Did any of the brothers have a pilot's license? Where were these brothers hiding now? And where was Janel's sister? Sawyer had killed one man already. Karla needed to be here, at the ranch, for her own protection and Janel's peace of mind.

Cole's name showed up on Zach's vibrating cell phone. They had been sharing information back and forth since Janel discovered the murderer's name. "Tell me you have good news."

"These are definitely our guys," Cole rattled off. "Oscar Sloan shared a prison cell with our murdered landscaper for a few months. The rest of his time, he bunked with a low-level member of a Mexican cartel, who smuggled drugs into Arizona through tunnels. I'm hoping no one from the cartel shows up around here."

"Me, too. Anything else?"

"An officer in Casa Grande swung by the apartment Oscar shares with the third brother, Larry. According to the manager, they've been gone for a few weeks."

Zach smiled at Janel. "We are so close to making an arrest, I can feel it in my bones."

Cole cleared his throat. "Unfortunately, I also have bad news."

"What now?"

When Janel raised her brows, Zach shrugged. "That Scottsdale detective called. He's at the gallery with Hyde. They have a warrant and want to see both sisters. It looks like a repeat of yesterday. I'm stuck at the station, so I won't be able to meet you there. Call me later."

"Will do." Zach hung up, anger twisting in his gut. He knew Hyde wouldn't let things drop. He was like a dog with a rawhide bone. "Let's go," he told Janel. "I'll explain on the way."

"What are we driving? We're fresh out of vehicles."

"The sheriff's office towed my loaner off the switchbacks and replaced the tire. Lieutenant Yeager dropped it off while you were sleeping, along with a warning not to drive it into a gunfight."

"As if we did it on purpose." Janel rolled her eyes, then grabbed her phone and purse on the way out the back door.

Checking for shooters and helicopters, Zach ushered Janel to the car, determined to keep her safe. Although, he knew full well her greatest peril today could be the detective waiting for them and the insurance investigator who kept claiming the twins should be locked up.

When they arrived at the gallery, Lieutenant Yeager opened the door and stepped outside. Zach wasn't surprised. Local police usually served search warrants since they had jurisdiction. Janel's gallery was in both Sedona and the county he and the lieutenant worked for.

After removing the key from the ignition, Zach walked around the car to open Janel's door. Her clenched hands showed her nervousness. Once they reached the sidewalk, she stood between the two men.

Zach asked his lieutenant, "Did they complete the search of the gallery yet?"

"They did. There was nothing to find." Yeager addressed Janel. "Miss Newman, where is your sister?"

"I don't know." When he looked doubtful, she repeated more forcefully. "I don't know. And why does it matter? This is my gallery. Her name isn't on it."

Lieutenant Yeager's gaze shifted to Zach. "They have an arrest warrant for Karla Newman."

"What?" Janel jerked back, bumping into Zach.

He grabbed her shoulders to hold her steady. "Let's take this conversation inside."

Seconds later, Zach found the Scottsdale detective and Hyde huddled in a corner beside a collection of framed watercolor paintings. When they spotted Janel, the detective whispered something to the insurance investigator.

Janel's assistant manager stood behind the counter, wrapping up a painted ceramic vase.

That explained how the lawmen gained access to the gallery.

Charlene gave them an apologetic look. "I know I was supposed to stay away, but that Hyde guy called and ordered me to come in. Can he do that?"

"We'll talk later," Janel told her.

Zach wondered where Charlene's boyfriend took off to. He was supposed to be her bodyguard.

When the detective crossed the room to speak to them, fury marred Janel's features. "Why are you trying to arrest my sister? She hasn't done anything wrong."

The smug look on Hyde's face had Zach's ire up once more. He reined in his emotions and focused on what the detective had to say.

"I'm sorry to tell you we've found a storage unit in Scottsdale rented in Karla's name." The detective casually placed his hands on his hips. "It contains artwork from each of the burglaries she was investigating this past year, along with printouts from her company showing their insured value."

Charlene's jaw dropped open.

Zach arched a brow. "Another anonymous tip?"

"Just good ole detective work." The detective narrowed his eyes at Zach. "I know how to do my job."

Janel crossed her arms over her chest. "Anyone could have rented that unit in her name, especially if the necessary paperwork was filled out online. It seems like you can do everything online these days."

The detective's features relaxed, as if remembering what Janel had been through recently. "There were containers inside with Karla's prints on them. They were on file because her employer required a background screening when they hired her."

"Tell her the best part," Hyde called out.

The detective sent him a dirty look.

They were playing a twisted version of good cop, bad cop.

"What?" Janel demanded.

The detective spoke to Zach. "I spoke to your brother this morning. He gave me Sawyer Sloan's name, and I called a gallery owner who was helping me with the case."

Hyde laughed. "Karla's been dating Sloan for a year now."

Zach felt like someone had pulled a rug out from under his feet. He reached for Janel, seeing the shock on her face.

"That's not true. She would have told me." Janel glared at Hyde. "My sister warned me about you. You'll twist the truth until she's out of the way so you can take her job."

"Your sister is telling fairy tales to cover up for her crimes."

"That's enough," Zach snapped at Hyde. "Detective, what proof do you have that they've been dating?"

"I only have the gallery owner's word, but I don't need to prove they were dating when I have her fingerprints connected to the stolen items."

"But not *on* the stolen items," Zach pointed out, "or you would have said so. Her fingerprints were on containers that could have been stolen from her house."

The detective worked his jaw. "I have enough evidence for a warrant. If you see her again, it's your responsibility to arrest her." To Janel, he added, "Just doing my job, ma'am."

"Not good enough." She fumed as she watched the detective head to the door. When Hyde was halfway across the room, she glared at him. "Don't ever come back to my gallery again."

Hyde smirked. "Your sister thinks she's smarter than me, but she isn't. I'm going to track her down and take great pleasure out of watching the cuffs tighten around her wrists. I might even snap a picture and send it to her supervisor."

"Out!" Zach demanded. How many times would he have to say that to this man? "Detective, *do not* bring him back here again."

Lieutenant Yeager marched to the door. "I'll make sure they leave."

Finally alone, except for Charlene, Zach felt a wave of regret flow over him. "Janel…" He looked into her wary face. The last thing he wanted to do was hurt her.

She shook her head, not wanting to hear what he would say, but he couldn't let that stop him.

"The detective is right. If I see Karla, I have to arrest her."

Janel felt her knees buckle beneath her, and Zach pulled her up into his arms. Remembering what he'd said, anger hit her like a punch to the gut. She backed up. "You're going to arrest my sister."

Zach's eyes begged her to understand. "I don't have a choice."

"Everyone has a choice." She spun away from him and marched over to Charlene, needing to be with someone who had her back. "I'm so glad to see you, but where's Robert?"

"He had to show a house in Prescott. He'll be back soon."

Janel couldn't bring herself to look over her shoulder at Zach. Everything was such a mess. He had kissed her and wanted to date, but she was keeping a big secret from him—she saw Karla with Sawyer Sloan, and now she had to face the fact her sister may have dated him. But would she have taken part in the burglary? Janel didn't want to think so.

Her headache returned as her mind spun with conflicting thoughts. Karla knew about Janel's bank loan and was worried about losing their mother's paintings, too. But her sister wasn't even in town when Mr. Allen asked Charlene to mail the painting he bought to Florida. She wouldn't have known about the potential hiding place. And she was too smart to leave a stolen painting out in the open in their mother's studio.

Was Sawyer in the gallery that day? Could he have heard Mr. Allen? Janel rubbed her forehead, wishing the answers would come to her. Instead, she pictured Karla in the parking lot with Sawyer. Why did she try to slap him? They didn't look like two people who liked one another.

Before she dared to speak, she checked to see where Zach stood. He was peering through the blinds, no doubt searching for the Sloan brothers and giving her space to cool off.

Janel whispered to Charlene, "Have you seen Karla lately?"

She glanced at Zach before answering in an equally hushed tone. "She dropped by my house last night, wanting to know where I bought the *malasadas* I sometimes bring to the gallery."

Karla was supposed to be fixing things, and she wanted to know about Portuguese donuts? "Did she tell you why she wanted to know?"

"Not last night. But during one of her visits, I brought in a dozen *malasadas*, and she said a man she occasionally dated had one every morning since his first trip to Hawaii. They're quite popular there. That's where I first tried one."

Zach strode toward the back of the gallery, sending them a questioning look. Janel pushed away nagging feelings of guilt as he passed by. Karla was her twin; she had to keep her out of jail. Whatever it took.

"What did you tell Karla?" Anticipation swelled in Janel's chest. This could be the first genuine lead to finding her sister before the Scottsdale detective or Hyde did.

"Sugary Joy Bakery in Flagstaff."

Janel pressed her lips together, hard. She didn't want to ask, but she had to know. "Did Karla give you the name of the man?"

"No. She only said she met him on a case." Charlene shrugged. "That's all I know."

"Thank you for your help." Janel wasn't sure if she should be relieved or disappointed that she didn't name Sawyer. "Please do me one more favor and don't tell anyone else about the bakery. No one at all. Unless directly asked by someone with a badge. I don't want you breaking the law."

After Charlene promised to keep their secret, Janel looked around, wondering what to do now. Putting all the pieces together, she could only conclude that her sister had sometimes dated Sawyer and planned to track him down using his weakness for *malasadas*.

Janel stepped away and pulled her phone out

of her purse. She checked her family locator app for her sister's whereabouts. *No location found.* Karla must have her phone turned off. After texting her to call back, she asked Charlene if she could borrow her car.

"No, you cannot borrow her car," Zach stated from the hallway leading to her office. "Someone is trying to kill you, remember?"

"Zach, what would you do if someone was trying to frame Lily? Would you hide at the ranch, or prove her innocence?"

He expelled a long breath. "I would prove her innocence, but you cannot do that without me. I've been the only thing between you and a bullet since you were running in the forest."

"But you'll arrest my sister."

"I was thinking about that." He drew closer, his presence formidable. "If I see her, I can hand her over to Cole, who doesn't have to call the Scottsdale detective immediately."

Hope sprung in her chest. "Your brother would buy us time?"

"If we're close to real evidence proving her innocence."

The gallery phone rang, and Charlene reached for it.

"We're closed," Janel reminded her. When the machine answered, she waited for a message or disconnect. The room grew quiet, and she heard the hum of traffic and a horn honk in the background.

Charlene read the caller ID. "Unknown caller. It's probably nothing." Her shaky voice belied her words.

Zach marched around the counter and snatched the receiver. "Who is this?" The line died. He hung up, and the message machine disconnected. Next, he tried dialing star sixty-nine. No one answered.

A shudder reverberated down Janel's spine. "Do you think that was Sawyer or one of his brothers?"

"Do you really want to hang around to find out?" Zach didn't wait for an answer. He turned to Charlene. "Leave now. If you're followed, call 911 and head straight to the police station. And don't come back here. *I mean it.*"

"I won't. If Hyde calls me again, I'll hang up," Charlene promised. She grabbed the box holding the vase she had prepared for shipping and Zach escorted her to her car.

Zach locked the back door and strode toward Janel. "Let's go."

"To Flagstaff. I have a lead."

Lines creased his forehead. "How did you find a lead?"

"I'll explain on the way."

Letting the subject drop for now, he stepped outside to make sure the front parking lot was clear. He waved to her, and she locked the door with swift movements. Seconds later, she was securing her seat belt in the passenger seat of his sheriff's vehicle.

He turned onto the main street, then spared a glance in her direction. "Did Karla tell you she was dating Sloan?"

"She usually meets guys online or at the gym. There wasn't anyone serious, and she only mentioned a guy if she had a funny story to tell. No one was named Sawyer."

"And Karla never mentioned dating someone she met on a case?" He glanced in the rearview mirror and then switched lanes.

"No. I wouldn't have approved if the case was still open." Janel had always been a rule follower—until now. Technically, she was interfering with an investigation by not telling Zach she remembered seeing her sister with Sawyer. But if he knew, he might assume Karla was guilty and not help prove her innocence.

Janel's stomach knotted, making her feel sick. Then she noticed Zach kept glancing in the mirror. "What's wrong?"

"We have company."

FIFTEEN

Alarmed, Janel twisted in her seat to look out the back window and then peered into her side mirror. "The black Ford Taurus? It was parked near the gallery."

"It's Hyde and the Scottsdale detective. They must think we'll lead them to Karla." While remaining in the right lane, he checked his side mirror. "I have a plan."

"That's good. We need one." She turned to face the back window again. There were three cars between them and the Ford. "Do you think they called the gallery to get us to leave? If so, it worked."

"Them or one of the Sloan brothers, trying to find you."

"I'm so tired of all of this. I'll never complain about being bored again."

"I can get behind that sentiment." He checked his mirrors again. "Prepare for sudden moves."

She adjusted her seat belt and reached for the car's grab handle. "Ready."

With the light turning yellow, Zach quickly switched lanes and, after entering the intersection, made a sudden U-turn.

Now traveling in the opposite direction, Janel watched the cars in front of Hyde and the detective stop at the red light. "They'll be stuck for a few minutes."

"Enough time to lose them."

"Maybe you should drive faster," Janel suggested.

Zach chuckled. "When we reach the interstate." He turned right into a residential neighborhood, left at the next corner and then right again two blocks later. This route took them to a back road. "Where did you plan to go in Charlene's car?"

After a slight hesitation, she told him Karla asked about a special donut. "Someone she occasionally dated has *malasadas* for breakfast every morning."

"You mean Sawyer," Zach concluded.

Janel sighed. "I'm going with that assumption. She wouldn't have gone to Charlene's house to ask about these donuts if some other guy she dated liked them."

"You're right. It sounds like Karla's hunting down the Sloan brothers."

"Yeah." Worry dripped from her one-word answer. Janel looked out the window, keeping an eye out for the Sloans, Karla, Hyde and the Scottsdale detective. She pulled her coat closed, the chill in the air growing as the outside temperature dipped. A light dusting of snow fell on the windshield, and Zach turned up the heater.

While they drove, Cole called with an update. There was an all-points bulletin out for the car Karla was driving. That would make it harder for her to remain free long enough to find Sawyer. Janel felt conflicted. She wanted her sister to find her proof, but being arrested might keep her alive. The Sloan brothers were dangerous men.

Zach glanced her way. Janel frowned but remained silent. What could she possibly say that would help her sister now? Nothing. If she told him she remembered seeing Karla trying to slap Sawyer, it would only make matters worse. It proved they were together in Sedona. If she told Zach her feelings for him were growing, he'd eventually learn she was hiding a memory and accuse her of using him. The best thing she could do was emotionally disconnect from him and focus on finding her sister.

They were entering Flagstaff when she noticed the blue helicopter flying high in the distance. "Not again."

"What?" Zach peered out through the window while the wipers swished back and forth, sweeping away the snow.

"Helicopter." Her tone hitched with fear. "It could be carrying a photographer or—"

"A shooter," he said, completing her thought.

"If they see us go into the bakery, they'll figure out we're close to finding them."

"That could put the employees there in danger. These men kill witnesses." Zach scanned their surroundings. "We need a place to hide the car."

"The university has parking garages."

"That will do." He turned onto East McConnell Drive while calling in another update to his lieutenant. "I need an unmarked car." They coordinated their plan and then disconnected.

The helicopter hovered over downtown Flagstaff. Why? Could the pilot be searching for them? If so, how did he know they were here? What if the Sloans spotted Karla? Would they kill her?

Zach entered the garage and drove up a level to hide his sheriff's vehicle. He parked and turned to Janel. "You okay?"

"I think so." The dread she heard in her own voice told a different story. "How can we put these horrible men in prison before they kill me or Karla if Hyde, a detective and possibly a helicopter pilot are searching for us?"

"One step at a time." Zach placed his hand over hers.

His touch felt warm and reassuring. "You said God sometimes shakes us out of our everyday life to force us to choose a new path."

"More or less."

"When does the shaking part stop?" Her voice cracked as she pushed back tears.

He squeezed her fingers. "You're not alone."

"I appreciate all you've done…even if I don't deserve your kindness." Remembering the secret she kept from him, she felt guilty and pulled her hand back into her lap.

"Janel…" The hum of an engine entering their level forced him to look away. Lieutenant Yeager parked a black SUV behind them and climbed out. Zach turned to her. "Time to go. We'll talk later."

They exited the marked sheriff's vehicle, and the two men exchanged car keys. Zach gestured toward their new ride. "Thanks for this."

"It has four-wheel drive. You might need it if the snow keeps falling." The lieutenant's gaze swept to Janel and back. "Do you want me to take Miss Newman to the ranch so you can follow this lead?"

"No." Janel panicked, taking a giant step away from the lieutenant. "Zach needs my help. Karla stormed out of our house after the search warrant. She won't listen to anyone but me."

"Then find her and talk fast," the lieutenant ordered, as if she worked for him. "Sawyer will do anything necessary to stay out of prison." He turned to Zach. "I paid a visit to his ex-wife. She lives near here. They have a six-year-old son, suffering from severe aplastic anemia."

"That's horrible." Janel couldn't imagine the depths of this woman's fear.

Yeager nodded his agreement. "Sawyer was helping her consult with specialists for the best course of treatment."

"No wonder the attacks have been relentless." Zach's expression filled with sympathy as he pushed back the brim of his Stetson. "When was the last time Sloan visited his son?"

"The day before the burglary at Miss Newman's gallery." The lieutenant opened the door to the marked sheriff's vehicle Zach had been driving. "I'll give you a head start. Someone might be watching for this vehicle to come out of the garage."

Janel and Zach climbed into the SUV and drove away. Trepidation built by the second. Finding the bakery was the easy part. What happened after that might get them killed.

Zach phoned his brother. "Cole, I need you to meet me in Flagstaff. I'll tell you why when you get here."

Janel lifted a brow.

"We might need backup, and I couldn't ask Yeager. He'd have to arrest Karla and hand her over to the Scottsdale detective."

"I'm surprised your lieutenant didn't mention the warrant."

"Me, too. But then, the burglaries are being handled by detectives outside of the sheriff's office. We want Sawyer for murder, and Karla could make our job easier."

Satisfied with his answer, Janel changed the subject. "I found the bakery on my phone. Turn right on Milton."

They stayed alert for signs of danger and for Karla while Janel navigated. Ten minutes later, they parked in front of Sugary Joy Bakery. The purple building stood out from the pine trees growing in the undeveloped areas around the quaint shop. Snow accumulating on the surrounding landscape and on the half dozen cars in the lot gave the scene a winter wonderland appearance, even though the feeling in the SUV was anything but enchanting.

"I'm going in with you," Janel stated flatly. "No offense, but I think it'll be easier for me to get information."

"No offense taken. Just don't say anything alarming. If Sawyer's been here, deputies will set up surveillance to capture him when he comes back. If the bakery staff looks scared, it will tip him off."

They strode to the entrance through the crisp air, hugging their coats tightly to stay warm. He tugged the door open and held it for her. The neatly decorated cakes in the window and the aroma of baked goods wafting through the air had her stomach grumbling.

They were perusing the offerings in the refrigerated display case when a college-aged teen, wearing pink glossy lipstick, black pants and a purple shirt sporting the store's logo, strolled over.

"Do you have any *malasadas*?" Janel asked, keeping her tone conversational.

"We do." The teen pointed to a tray in the top left row, then suddenly did a double take. "You look familiar. Didn't you buy some this morning?"

"You're thinking of my twin sister. She might have been here with this guy." Janel showed her the picture of Sawyer.

"He's been in here a few times, but they were never together."

"Really?" Janel's mood lightened, and she pointed to the display case. "We'll take half a dozen *malasadas*. Two of each flavor and two coffees."

While the girl bagged their order, Zach joined the conversation. "Did you see which direction he drove from? We're trying to find her sister so we can give her a ride back to Sedona."

"They broke up," Janel explained. "She doesn't want to be near him. You know how it is."

"Been there." The teen snatched two cups and filled them with coffee. "All I know is the man in the picture walked over here from that hotel." She pointed to a building half a block away.

"Thank you for your help." Janel took the bag and cups over to a counter containing creamer and sugar to prepare their coffee. Zach finished paying and then held the door open for her.

Outside, on the way out to the car, she grinned. "Admit it, I did good."

"Yes, you did. Now we call in the deputies." He clicked the doors open.

"Not yet." She climbed inside the SUV and waited for him to join her. "We have to find Karla first."

He met her stern gaze with his own. "What if Sawyer sees *you* first?"

After a fifteen-minute debate, Zach had relented and agreed to finding Karla before they called in the deputies. He parked the SUV in front of a nearby diner to wait for Cole. "There he is."

"Thanks." Janel sent Zach an apologetic look. "I know I'm not making this easy for you."

He blew out a long breath, remembering what his parents always said about looking at a situation from another's perspective. "I have a sister, too, and if Lily were caught up in this mess, I'd do anything to help her."

"I knew you'd understand," Janel said, her tone sincere. "And I pray Lily will always be safe."

Cole parked and walked over to their open driver's side window. It took only a minute to fill him in on recent developments. He whistled and pushed back the brim of his felt cowboy hat. "You're in a pickle. You can't go into the hotel without backup, and we can't leave Janel in the car alone."

"And I promised not to call in the deputies until after we find Karla." Zach frowned, wishing this case wasn't so difficult to navigate. He prayed for guidance, then took a leap of faith. "Let's play it by ear."

"Now, why didn't I think of that?" Cole's sarcastic tone hung in the air.

"We can't make a plan until we see the layout of the hotel, anyway."

"True." Cole opened the back door of the SUV. "We'll be less conspicuous if we arrive in one car."

Zach turned the key to start the engine, then noticed Janel's blond locks. "These guys are less likely to notice you if your hair is inside your coat's hood."

She quickly obliged. "And you two wouldn't stick out from the crowd if you ditched the cowboy hats."

"Good point." Zach handed his hat to his brother in the back seat, then ran his hand through his hair to straighten it out and noticed Janel was watching with interest.

A few minutes later, he drove the SUV around the hotel, a three-story beige building with white trim. The snow-covered grounds appeared neatly kept. Not first-class accommodation, but not run-down, either.

"I'm not seeing any familiar vehicles." Zach scanned the parking lot once more. "Definitely no motorcycles."

"How do you want to play this?" Cole asked.

"I have jurisdiction, so I'll go inside." Zach turned in his seat to speak directly to his brother. "How about you sit up here and watch over Janel? If Sawyer shows up, call me."

After Cole agreed to the plan, Zach flipped Janel's visor down to block part of her face, then handed her the sunglasses he'd stashed in his coat pocket. The car would get stuffy if they couldn't keep the heavily tinted windows open a crack.

Cole took his place behind the driver's seat and opened the bag of *malasadas* sitting on the center console. The enticing aroma wafted through the air.

Zach strode inside the office, where he found a middle-aged woman bundled up in a sweater behind the registration desk. According to her name tag, she was the hotel manager.

"Good evening, Molly." He showed her his badge, then the picture of Sawyer he'd saved on his phone. "Have you seen this man?"

"We run a respectable establishment here." Her voice remained flat as she stared at the picture.

"I'll take that as a yes. Which room?"

"Twenty. Bottom floor on the end." She swiped a key card through a machine and handed it to him. "You can let yourself in."

"When was the last time you saw him?"

"He sped out of here with his buddies about two hours ago." She pulled up the registration information on her computer, wrote it down, including vehicle make, model and license plate, then handed it over.

Zach showed her the mug shot for Oscar Sloan. "Is this one of his buddies?"

She groaned and nodded. "An ex-con. Figures. He shaved off that hideous goatee, but it's him."

"And this one?" Zach pulled up the military picture for Larry Sloan.

"He's with the other two. At least he doesn't have a mug shot."

"Not yet." He wanted to know if Karla and Sawyer were still dating, but he didn't have a picture of her. A thought occurred to him, and he brought up a picture from the gallery website. The sisters looked so much alike that one of Janel might work. "How about this woman? Was she with these men?"

"She showed me a picture of the first guy. Said he was her brother."

"Did you give her a key card, too?"

"Absolutely not. I gave her his room number, nothing else. I don't want any trouble here."

"Let's hope you don't get any." He strode out the door and over to Cole, who rolled down the window.

Janel leaned across the seat. "Did you learn anything useful?"

Zach lifted the key card for them to see. "They're not here." He gave his brother the piece of paper the woman had written on. "If this car returns, don't waste a second calling me. I'm going to check out the room."

He strode across the wet asphalt to room twenty and let himself inside what turned out to be a two-bedroom suite. The living area was neat and clean. Surprising for three criminals. Each bed held open suitcases, packed and ready to go. *Prepared for a quick getaway, or leaving town soon?*

The manager had given him permission to go into the room, but that did not extend to searching through suitcases. Heading back into the main area, he surveyed the couch, coffee table, television and desk. Something felt out of place.

Looking up, he noticed there were two smoke detectors on the ceiling. One above the coffee maker, and one close to the desk. Hotels wouldn't have two detectors in one room.

He pulled out the desk chair and climbed on top, suspecting the detector above was a spy camera. It took little effort to yank it off the ceiling and find the recorder hidden inside. He'd seen one of these before. If Karla planted it, the digital recording would be sent to her phone, or any other device she'd selected.

After placing it on the desk, he called his lieutenant, who enthusiastically reported that he would call for backup and work on obtaining a search warrant.

Zach returned to the SUV and discovered Janel was already excited. She didn't even know about the fake smoke detector yet. "What's up?"

"My sister showed up on my app." She lifted her phone for him to see. "We have to go back to my house—now."

When Zach told them about the recording device, Cole agreed to wait in the office for the deputies to arrive and pocketed the hotel key card. Climbing out of the driver's seat, he added, "It makes sense to take her back to Sedona. Yeager would agree. He told you to keep her safe."

He thanked his brother with a tap on his shoulder and then took his seat behind the wheel.

"Let's hurry." Janel buckled up her seat belt.

"First, tell me how long you've had a location finder on your phone."

When he raised a brow, she scowled. "Don't give me that look. It only works if her phone is turned on, which it wasn't until a few minutes ago."

"Did you call her?"

"I tried. She didn't answer." Janel pointed to the key in the starter. "Let's go before she leaves—or the Sloan brothers find her. Somehow, they know everything."

SIXTEEN

Janel warmed her hands in front of the SUV's heating vent. They were ten miles away from her house. "Can you drive faster?"

"The sun's gone down. It's dark and snowy." Zach glanced at the rearview mirror.

"You're right. I'm just so worried about my sister."

"We're almost there. Try focusing on the good news. We have witnesses who can say Karla wasn't hanging around Sawyer and his brothers. The teen in the bakery said they never came in together, and the manager said Karla had to show his picture and ask for a room number. If they were still dating, he would have called her from a burner phone. That puts doubt in the theory that she was in on your burglary."

Janel studied his face as the light from oncoming traffic illuminated his strong features. "Then you believe we were both framed, not just me?"

He spared her a glance before returning his attention to the slippery roads. The windshield wipers swished as they swiped away the sleet. "Yes, I truly believe you're both innocent."

Relief flowed through her. "Then there's something I should tell you. I hated keeping it a secret, but I had to, for Karla's sake. It made her look guilty when I knew in my heart she wasn't."

This time, he kept his eyes on the road. "I'm listening."

Janel couldn't tell from his voice what he was thinking. After hesitating, she decided there was no backing down now. "I remembered seeing Karla outside a café in Sedona the morning the landscaper died. She tried to slap Sawyer. I didn't know his name then. They argued and drove away in separate cars. I knew she wouldn't tell me what happened because she never wanted me to worry. Then I remembered seeing Sawyer in the gallery and suspected he'd been casing the gallery."

Zach pulled over onto the road's unpaved shoulder, and she could sense his mixed emotions through his stiffening posture. "When exactly did you remember seeing this?"

"At the house. After they found my mother's painting." She felt like an invisible wall protecting her from the bad guys was crumbling away. "Don't hate me, please."

"Of course, I don't hate you." He huffed a heavy breath. "And when you confronted Karla, what did she have to say for herself?"

"She said she was going to fix things." Janel

realized too late that her statement would erase his belief in Karla's innocence. "My sister *did not* steal from anyone. That predator targeted her to keep tabs on the investigation. There is no doubt in my mind."

"I thought you didn't trust your instincts?"

Anger struck her like lightning. "How dare you throw that in my face?"

"Make me understand, Janel. You withheld vital information. We could have talked to Karla at the house, discovered exactly what we were up against and solved this case by now. You are still in danger because of your sister."

"Don't say that." Conflicting feelings warred inside her. "She's fixing this."

"What else are you hiding?"

"Nothing. I swear."

"Omitting the truth is a lie. You've been lying to me." He clenched his jaw, then drew in a calming breath and met her gaze. "Didn't our kiss mean anything?"

"It meant everything." She wiped a tear from her cheek. "But Karla is my blood. My twin. I had to know you would believe in her innocence before I could share this."

"What I know is relationships are built on trust. And we don't have any." He angrily drove back onto the main road, not giving her another look.

Her slashed heart sunk irretrievably into a bottomless pit.

"Everyone keeps secrets, Zach. Even you," she shot back. "Your job requires it."

"That's different."

"Not from where I'm sitting. You keep secrets to protect the innocent, and so did I." She stared out the window, wondering how long it would take for Sawyer and his brothers to return to the hotel where they would be arrested. Once that happened, she could return home for good. Not a minute too soon.

She might also have to start attending a new church. Entering through the same doors, expecting to see him and then knowing he didn't want to see her would hurt too much.

God, why is this happening? Please tell me what to do. Show me. I need Your help.

They drove in silence until Zach slowed in front of her house. Her mother's sedan had been abandoned at the entrance to the driveway, the back end still on the street.

"Karla's still here." Janel waited impatiently for the SUV to come to a full stop near the street-light, then she flung open the door.

"Wait!" Zach rushed around the front of the car, following her.

Janel ran along the bushes lining their large snowy yard, stopping only to inspect the sedan's back tire. Most of the tread was missing. Her sister must have kept driving on the flat to get here, then left it parked over fifty feet from the house. The need to see her sister overtook her. She rushed toward the front door, following the single set of footprints in the snow.

Karla always locked the door, so Janel quickly searched through her purse and retrieved the key. Standing beneath the porch light, she was about to insert it into the lock when she detected the faint scent of rotten egg.

Zach stepped onto the porch, then suddenly grabbed her arm and pulled her into a full run down the driveway.

"Let me go! My sister's in there." Exasperated, she tried to yank free. "Karla!"

Gunshots followed the hum of an engine on the street.

"Down!" Zach pushed her behind the bushes lining the yard and dove on top of her. Snow-covered grass cushioned her face as she listened.

The Sloans were here to kill them.

More gunshots. One took out a window.

The earth suddenly shook below them.

A roar from the house breathed life into an explosion, ripping through the air.

The car sped away, and Zach rolled off her back. She pushed to her hands and knees and stared up at the flames that engulfed her house. Heat from the raging fire flowed through the air above them.

"Karla!" Pushing to her feet, she scanned the yard, desperately searching the shadows for her sister. Tears choked her. She coughed on the smoke and irrepressible misery. "Where are you?"

Zach grabbed hold of her arm. "We have to go!"

Firelight flickered over his face. Janel stared at him, unable to speak or move. Her sister was dead because of her. Everything was her fault. She was the only witness. This explosion was meant for her.

"Janel, they could come back. I'll call the lieutenant, but we have to leave. Now!"

Minutes after receiving a text from Charlene, asking for their help, Zach parked the SUV in front of her quaint one-story house, only feet away from the concrete driveway where the assistant manager's red two-door coupe sat. Like the other homes in this older neighborhood, a solitary oak tree—missing its leaves—grew in the center of the snow-covered yard.

During their drive, Zach had tried to come up with a scenario where Karla was still alive. "Maybe your sister took a rideshare or walked to a neighbor's house," he suggested, removing the key from the ignition.

Janel continued to stare out the passenger side window, her body limp like a doll. "Footprints. They show Karla walked to the door and never came back out."

She was right. There had been only one set

of footprints. They led from the car Karla was
driving to the porch. Not back again. What both-
ered Zach was the amount of gas that had filled
the house. Karla would have smelled it—unless
she'd been asleep, unconscious or dead. The Sloan
brothers could have killed her and then blew up
the house to destroy the evidence.

The front door suddenly swung open, and
Charlene, illuminated by the porch light, ran outside.

"Something horrible must have happened."
Janel sprang from the SUV, then slammed the
door shut.

Zach rushed to join the women on the sidewalk.
Charlene was talking so fast he couldn't understand what she was saying. "I need you to start
at the beginning and speak slower."

Charlene pressed a hand to her chest and inhaled deeply. "I heard someone in my backyard
and called Robert, but he's stuck in Prescott. His
tire blew out. He told me to call the police."

"Good advice." Zach scanned the front of the
house and then grabbed a flashlight before walking over to the side gate to examine the lock. It
was still secure. "Could have been raccoons."

She shook her head. "I know the difference
between animals trying to get into the trash and
a human walking over my backyard river rock."

"What did the 911 dispatcher say?"

"I was on the phone with her when I heard an

explosion. I reported that, too. She told me an officer would be out, but I know whatever blew up will probably take precedent. They might not be here for hours." Charlene's brows furrowed when she turned toward Janel, who held fingers over her mouth as tears flowed down her cheeks. "Did something happen?"

"There was a gas leak at her house." Zach placed his hand gently on Janel's arm, but he knew there was no comforting her. Her grief was too deep.

Charlene's eyes grew big. "Your house…blew up?"

Janel nodded. "Karla…" Devastated, she couldn't say more.

"Karla's car was parked out front," Zach explained. "We believe she was inside when it happened."

"No!" Charlene gathered Janel into a big hug. "I'm so sorry. Please, come inside. We can sit while Zach checks my backyard."

"I prefer you both sit in the SUV until I come back." He waited for them to climb into the front seats before he clicked the doors locked with his key fob. His footfalls crunched the snow, and he could see his breath in the air as he strode toward the house.

After pushing the door fully open, he slowly stepped into the living room. A blue sofa, rocking chair and television took up most of the small space. He had to go through the kitchen to enter the backyard. An enticing aroma wafted from the Crock-Pot, reminding him they hadn't stopped for dinner yet. Janel needed to eat something more substantial than donuts before long.

While opening the back door, he discovered it was unlocked. He considered it odd for a woman living alone and hearing noises outside. Concern stiffened his spine as the beam of his flashlight pierced the darkness.

More troubling were the footprints in the snow, leading from the backyard wall to the concrete porch. Zach pulled out his weapon and methodically checked each room of the house, the hairs on his neck standing on end.

No one hid behind a door, under a bed or in a closet. But the room in the far corner of the house felt colder than the others. Gun ready, he pushed aside the drapes covering an open window. On the ground outside were more footprints in the snow. The intruder had escaped over the brick wall four feet away.

Remembering Janel and Charlene were waiting in the SUV, fear pumped through his arteries. He ran down the hall, through the living room and out through the front door.

The women were still there waiting for him. He lifted his finger, signaling for them to wait. He then crept closer to the car in the driveway. Footprints illuminated by the streetlight showed the intruder had jumped from the wall that surrounded the yard, into the snow, then walked down the sidewalk to the street where the trail disappeared, mostly likely erased by neighborhood traffic.

Zach strode over to the SUV. When Janel rolled down the driver's side window, he shared what he'd discovered. "Charlene," he began, leaning to the side to see her in the passenger seat. "When did you hear someone in the backyard?"

"Maybe ten minutes before I texted you two. Why?"

He glanced about one more time. "That was at least twenty minutes ago. Your intruder is probably long gone. Come on in. See if anything is missing."

Back inside the house, Zach and Janel followed Charlene from room to room. It wasn't until she reached the kitchen that she noticed anything odd.

"This wasn't here when I heard the noise outside, and it isn't mine." Charlene picked up the cell phone, protected by a teal-colored case, resting on top of a receipt on the kitchen counter next to the refrigerator. Her motions caused the receipt to fall to the tile floor.

Janel reached out for the device. "It's Karla's." Surprise, then confusion, flashed across her face. "How did it get here?"

He picked up the grocery store receipt and noticed writing on the back. He read it to the others.

"'Give my phone to Janel and tell her to avoid the house. Natural gas leak—already reported. PS, I need to borrow your car. Thanks, Karla.'"

Janel's eyes sparked with joy. "That's her handwriting. She's alive!"

Zach was at a loss for words. Relieved, he sent her a warm smile. Apparently, Karla had smelled natural gas like they had. Because of her car's flat tire, she couldn't drive anywhere. "But we didn't see footprints leaving the porch."

"We have pavers between the porch and the water spigot," Janel noted. "We didn't walk over there to check for footprints."

"My car keys are missing!" Charlene stood in front of a Home Sweet Home mail and key holder hanging on the kitchen wall above the light switch.

They all rushed out to the front yard and discovered the red coupe was gone.

"How did we not hear her leave?" Janel ran to the sidewalk and searched the street.

Charlene shrugged. "Karla probably left when my neighbor came home." She pointed to a sports car in the driveway next to hers. "I heard him."

So did Zach, although faintly. Charlene had good insulation in her house.

Janel appeared to accept the explanation, but then her brow creased. "If Karla just left, she was hiding from us. I don't get it." Her gaze locked on Zach's. "Is it because you're here and there's a warrant for her arrest? I mentioned it in one of my text messages."

"I forgot about the warrant." Snowflakes fell on Charlene's green sweater, and she swiped them away. "Let's go back inside. It's cold out here."

Zach shared his thoughts with Janel as they walked back to the house. "Karla left you the phone for a reason."

"I know her password. Let's hurry." Janel's dedication to putting the Sloan brothers behind bars had returned full force.

"I'll put a kettle on. I have tea and hot chocolate," Charlene offered, not appearing overly concerned about her car. She must have faith she'd get it back.

Inside the warm kitchen, Zach sat beside Janel at a round wooden table while she entered her sister's password. Charlene kept herself busy, pulling mugs from the cupboard and prepping their drinks as if wanting to give them privacy.

"I think I found something." Janel squinted while checking the phone's app. She tapped on one image, then another. "This looks like a recording from the camera hidden in the fake hotel smoke detector."

Zach leaned closer to view the screen. The video started with the profile view of Sawyer Sloan typing on a laptop. A man off-screen groaned. "I don't know why we ever listened to you. Faking a break-in to get close to that woman was the worst idea you ever had."

Sawyer shook his head. "You don't know what you're talking about. Karla was investigating our heists. She told me everything, and I led her in the wrong direction."

"Right," the man scoffed.

"You're an idiot. I was the one who suggested she look into art thieves released from prison over the past five years, especially ones on the East Coast, where there are more museums and wealthy investors. Remember when I told you she thought some guy out of Boston might be guilty?" Sawyer looked up from the screen as if waiting for an answer that never came, so he went on. "Dating her also gave me easy access to her spare house key. You wouldn't have been able to put those bags with her fingerprints in the storage shed if it weren't for me."

"Okay, okay," the man mumbled. "But you shouldn't have killed Red. He was a good guy."

Sawyer narrowed his eyes. "If your prison buddy was such a good guy, why did he pull a gun on me?"

"He doesn't think straight sometimes. You could have just roughed him up a bit and he would've got the message."

"Enough already." The third Sloan brother, Larry, pulled a chair up next to Sawyer at the desk. "We need to transfer enough money for me and Oz to leave the state."

"I'd have it done already if he'd kept his trap shut." Sawyer typed the name of an overseas bank into the search engine, slowly enough for Zach to see each keystroke.

Seconds later, Zach's eyes widened. Stolen art paid well. He grabbed his phone and snapped a picture. He knew Oscar, nicknamed Oz, was a petty thief, but this was a whole new level of criminality. A balance of over five million dollars sat in their account after they transferred three hundred thousand to a US bank for traveling expenses.

"You sure you don't want to go with us?" Larry asked Sawyer.

"I can't. My kid needs me."

The video abruptly ended, and Zach, feeling sorry for the sick boy, contacted Cole to tell him about the evidence they were forwarding from the two phones.

"I was just about to call you." Cole's tone sounded more serious than usual. "According to Hyde, Karla called him, told him about the overseas account and claimed she transferred those millions to the insurance company's bank account."

"Why?" Zach stepped away from the table, not yet ready to share this information with Janel. "What is she hoping to accomplish?"

"Hyde said she called Sawyer and left him a message. She had their money, and they could pick it up at the Mexican border—if they left her sister alone."

Zach pushed the rim of his Stetson away from his face. "Why call Hyde? She claims he's been wanting her job."

"I guess she was trying to prove she was one of the good guys by telling him he could arrange for the police to pick up the Sloan brothers at the border. Also, the insurance company would need to know where the money came from. And one more thing, she also told Hyde that you would soon have access to the video proving the Sloan brothers are guilty, not her and Janel."

"Remind me to thank her." Sarcasm dripped from Zach's words. "The last thing I need is Hyde on my tail." He noticed the impatient expression on Janel's face when he ended the call and told her, "We need to head back to the ranch."

Janel remained seated. "You were talking about my sister. I want to know what's going on."

His trepidation grew with each passing second. "Karla just gave Sawyer and his brothers a good reason to kidnap you—before they kill both you and your sister."

SEVENTEEN

Janel tried to figure out where her sister would go. She desperately wanted to search for her, rather than drive back to the ranch, but Zach had put his foot down. He was convinced the Sloan brothers would try to kidnap her, and he was probably right. They wanted their five million dollars back from Karla and could use her as leverage.

When they entered Zach's living room, Janel did a double take. Karla sat on the sofa, speaking to Cole, who took notes on a tablet.

Janel felt waves of emotion wash over her: relief, love, joy, anger, then exhaustion.

Karla strode over and pulled her into a hug. "I'm so glad you're okay. Cole said you went to the house. You could have died in the explosion."

She couldn't help but chuckle at the irony of her statement as a tear slid down her cheek. "I thought *you* did."

They hugged again, and Zach cleared his throat. "You have a lot of explaining to do, Karla."

"You're right." Karla stepped back. "I was giving my statement to Cole, but I'll start again."

"From the beginning." Zach's stern tone altered the mood in the room. He waited for Janel to join her sister on the sofa before he sat across from them, near his brother's chair.

The serious expressions on the men's faces made Janel feel the need to show her sister support. She placed her hand on top of Karla's.

A smile tugged at her sister's lips before she turned to the lawmen. "All right. Here we go, from the beginning. I met Sawyer Sloan when expensive pieces of his art collection were stolen from his house. I thought his break-in might be connected to a string of burglaries I was working on. A couple of weeks later, I ran into him at my gym. He asked me out. One thing led to another, and we started dating once or twice a month. I thought he was being nice when he offered to fix my kitchen faucet."

Janel groaned. "That must be when he stole your spare key."

"You listened to the recording on my phone." Karla's eyes lit with pride. "I knew you'd find it." She turned back to Cole. "Sawyer told me he had two brothers but claimed they lived in Texas. One day, I was running errands and spotted the three of them standing next to an SUV at a gas station. I could see the family resemblance in their nose shape and jawlines. He later lied about where he had been, and my suspicious nature took over."

"You discovered his brother has an arrest record," Zach concluded.

"Yes, for game store burglaries. He never became a person of interest during my initial investigation into the art burglaries, so I didn't memorize his last name." Karla took a sip from the water glass on the coffee table. "I started putting the pieces of the puzzle together, and a picture of Sawyer running a burglary ring with his brothers began to emerge. When the Scottsdale detective arrested the fence, I went to see him. I flat out asked if he bought the stolen merchandise from the Sloan brothers."

"Did you expect him to be honest with you?" Janel didn't know any criminals, but according to the television shows she watched, they usually lied.

"You never know for sure until you try. Unfortunately, I couldn't get a straight answer out of him, but then I didn't need to because he told Sawyer about our visit."

Janel's head ached again, just when she thought she had totally recovered from the concussion.

"Sawyer confronted me, and we argued. I accused him of using me, and he laughed." Karla shook her head. "He told me what a fool I had been to walk straight into their trap, which he spelled out. They rented a storage unit in my name and filled it with one piece of stolen art from each burglary, plus boxes and bags with my fingerprints and DNA on them. They framed me."

"And if you ratted on them, they'd make an anonymous call to the police," Zach guessed. He rubbed his chin with the pad of his finger. "Only you didn't rat on them, and they made the anonymous call to the Scottsdale detective, anyway."

Karla nodded. "When Janel witnessed Sawyer killing the redheaded accomplice, their plan crumbled. That's why they forced the fence to name both me and my sister as his source for the stolen art. They needed to discredit her before she could finger Sawyer as the killer."

"Which wouldn't have happened if my memories hadn't come back." There were a few times Janel wished she hadn't recalled those horrific moments.

"Sawyer showed me a video of you working at the gallery." Karla's expression filled with angst. "He threatened to kill you if the police ever questioned him."

Janel squeezed her sister's hand. "I don't blame you for not saying anything. You were afraid. I know how that feels."

"The argument I had with Sawyer, the one Janel remembered seeing, was about the gallery burglary. I believe he wouldn't have gone back to the casita for the stolen art so soon after hiding it

if I hadn't seen him in town and confronted him."
Karla directed her statements to Zach. "When I
saw him in the café parking lot, I accused him
of stealing our mother's paintings. He must have
thought I was wearing a wire because he kept
ranting about how I was crazy and probably stole
from my sister, and maybe Janel was in on it, too.
He knew about the loan and made disparaging re-
marks about her, so I tried to slap him."

Cole took more notes. "Why didn't you say
anything *after* Janel was almost killed in the forest and your car blew up?"

"You were convinced the gallery break-in
wasn't connected to the ring of burglaries. I
thought you were probably right. Sawyer wouldn't
have had Janel's security code to disable the
alarm, and to my knowledge, the Sloan brothers never murdered anyone before." Once again,
Karla spoke to Janel. "I wasn't positive Sawyer
was the one trying to kill you until you remembered seeing us together in the parking lot and
told me he was the murderer."

"Then you tried to make it all go away." Janel
wished her sister had asked Cole and Zach for
help.

"And you thought hiding a camera in their hotel
room, which gave you access to their bank password so you could transfer millions out of their
account, would fix things?" The remark was less
question and more sarcasm. An incoming call

on Cole's phone kept him from waiting for an answer.

Janel had to agree it might not have been the best move to make under the circumstances, but Karla did prove their innocence. A win in her book.

Zach scowled at Karla. "Don't you get it? There's no way they will leave the country without their money. And Sawyer won't leave at all. His son is too sick. They will do everything possible to kidnap Janel to force you to give back their money."

"Sawyer never told me he had a child." Karla turned her gaze away from the brothers. "Why would he? I was a means to an end." The hurt flickering across Karla's face made Janel think there might have been a time when her sister thought she had a future with Sawyer—before she realized he was a criminal.

The second Cole disconnected his call, Zach asked, "What now?"

"A no-name caller claims there's going to be an attack on the police station. He didn't say when. The chief asked the sheriff to send deputies over to help defend the place in case it comes to that."

"The Sloan brothers aren't planning to attack the police station," Zach concluded. "They're coming here instead."

"They can do both." The hospital explosion flashed through Janel's mind. "They have bombs."

"And grenades," Zach mumbled. "Probably from their Mexican drug cartel connection."

Cole stood. "Regardless, the priority is defending the police station. We won't get additional officers when we have three living on the ranch."

Janel vividly remembered the fear of running away from Sawyer in the forest and shooting at him from the bedroom window. The idea of facing off with him again sent terror pulsating down her spine. "I need more guns."

Sitting at the dining room table with Cole, Jackson, Lily and their parents, Zach reflected on the business the ranch had lost after his brothers inadvertently brought danger to it. He had been working hard to entice resort managers to recommend their hayrides and cowboy cookouts to their visitors ever since. Now this.

He brought Janel and her sister here because it was the right thing to do, even if another attack might bring their equine business to financial ruin. His unsteady nerves had him clenching his jaw as a solemn mood settled over him and his thoughts wandered.

Tombstone came to mind. Tourists flocked there to see the O.K. Corral. They had a gunfight in 1881 that lasted less than one minute. Admittedly, books and movies about Wyatt Earp made it more famous. Zach didn't see a movie deal in their future, but maybe a public relations person could help turn their bleak financial situation around—if he could find an alternative to bringing witnesses to the ranch in the future. Official law enforcement agencies hadn't made that possible yet.

Lily kept her laptop open in front of her so she could watch the security monitor during the meal their mother had kept warm until everyone came home. His sister could protect Janel and Karla as well as anyone else in the family.

"Zach." Cole placed his cell phone down beside his plate. "I spoke to Sierra, and we both agree you should hide the twins in our house since it's at the far end of the ranch and less likely to be noticed."

"She's sure about that?" Their father reached for a dinner roll. He had been a pillar of strength all their lives, but the years were showing in the wrinkles on his face and the gray streaks in his hair. "I can't believe any woman would want to come back from visiting relatives to find their house full of bullet holes."

"Yes, she's sure," Cole stated emphatically. "Sierra remembers when she needed help and wants to do the same for Janel and her sister."

Their mother tapped her husband's hand. "Where's your manners? Wait for our guests."

"We're going to battle. I need sustenance." He turned at the sound of footfalls in the hall. "There they are." He snatched another roll, and she rolled her eyes.

The twins joined them at the table, both dressed alike in black jeans and black turtleneck sweaters. Karla believed the Sloans wouldn't shoot Janel if they thought she might be the sister who could transfer their money back.

Janel chose the seat next to Zach, but their gazes didn't meet. His heart still struggled over his feelings for her. He meant what he said; he couldn't have a romantic relationship with someone who kept secrets. His ex did so before she went back to her old boyfriend. He refused to go through that again.

"Let's say grace," his mother said, her tone as light as the circumstances would allow.

They held hands, and his father began, "Lord, we ask Your blessing for this food, Your protection as we defend our home and Your strength to win the battle. Amen."

A chorus of "Amen" ended the prayer.

Zach silently asked God for guidance before reluctantly releasing Janel's hand. She was still his friend, and he worried over what the night had in store for her—for them all. "Lily, how does it look out there?"

"Quiet. No sign of trouble." Lily took her eyes off the laptop for five seconds to spoon mashed potatoes on her plate when Cole handed her the bowl.

Jackson stabbed a pork chop on the platter with

his fork. "Zach, you're in charge of protecting the twins. How do you want to handle this?"

"I was thinking you and Cole could stay here to watch over the house with Mom and Dad. They'll show up here looking for Janel. The rest of us can go to the other house."

"Solid plan," Cole confirmed, accepting the platter from Jackson.

His brothers had more law enforcement experience, so it meant a lot to Zach that they respected his opinion.

After dinner, Lily and Zach stashed weapons and phone chargers into a duffel bag while Janel and Karla thanked everyone for their help. The four of them then tugged on their coats before climbing into the unmarked sheriff's SUV. Zach drove them down the ranch road to Cole's house, which was nestled in a far corner, surrounded by evergreen trees. He parked inside the garage.

"Ladies, let's keep the blinds closed and the lights off." He pushed open the driver's door and carried the bag filled with guns and ammunition inside.

"Can I at least make coffee?" Lily placed her laptop on the table.

"Please do." Zach placed his arsenal on the kitchen table next to an unread newspaper, then traveled from room to room with a flashlight to reacquaint himself with his new surroundings. Peering out through each window, he was glad to see everything appeared normal. A blanket of snow covered the pasture beneath the starry night, while the horses stayed warm in their stalls. The thought of another assault endangering his serene home made him clench his teeth.

Minutes later, they sat at the table drinking coffee. The caffeine would help keep them alert. The laptop and a kitchen night-light provided minimum illumination. Shadows flickered on the wall, making them all jumpy.

"What do we do now?" Janel hugged the warm cup with both hands.

Her vulnerability tugged at his emotions. "We wait." He pushed a pistol in front of each twin. "Karla, do you know how to use this if anyone breaks in?"

She nodded. "I own a gun but didn't bring it with me."

After three hours and four cups of coffee, they moved to the living room, where they would be more comfortable. He relocated the night-light to the wall behind the dining room table so they could see more from any of the main rooms without drawing attention to the house. Janel placed her weapon on the coffee table, and so did Karla.

"Help me move the sofa away from the window." Zach started pushing once everyone found a place to stand and take hold of the frame. Preparing for another attack felt surreal. He'd spent months helping Cole build this house.

Lily sat on the carpet with her computer while the sisters claimed spots on the sofa. Zach moved an overstuffed chair into the corner and sat where he could see both entrances to the room and all three windows.

Time ticked by slowly. Janel crossed her arms over her chest, hiding her shaking hands. Eventually, she nodded off to sleep, then jerked awake again.

An hour later, Lily handed him the laptop. "I need to stretch."

"No problem." He placed the device on his thighs and took over, monitoring the ranch as his sister walked up and down the hallway.

After she returned to her spot on the carpet, the silence became deafening again.

Eventually, each of the women fell asleep.

Fear and suspense kept him alert.

When the first rays of morning light shone through the windows, Zach heard the whir of helicopter blades. He nudged Lily with her boot. "Wake up." When she peered up at him, he added, "We have company. Call Cole, then the sheriff's office."

Their voices woke Janel and Karla, and he instructed them to stay on the sofa.

Zach stood beside the window, peering out through the blinds at the helicopter flying with its door open over the stables. A man covered in black from head to toe climbed down a rope, with a rifle slung over his shoulder. He jumped onto the metal roof of one of the stables and then scrambled to the snow-covered ground.

"Watch them," Zach told Lily as he pulled out his Glock. "I'm headed to the stables." His gaze met Janel's.

Her eyes grew wide, and she snatched two pistols from the coffee table. He remembered she didn't want to stop shooting to reload.

"I'll be back. Do what Lily says." He grabbed his coat from the kitchen and snuck out through the back door. When he neared the pasture, two ATVs roared across the blanket of white, heading straight for the horses, now galloping out of the stables. The drivers wore helmets that covered their faces, but there was no secret behind who had invaded the ranch.

Zach's ire threatened to take control of his mind and actions. *No.* The voice in his head was his, but the thought felt like God sent it—a reminder to stay on the right path.

When Zach caught up with his brothers halfway between the two houses, he announced, "I'm going to the stables to deal with that guy."

Jackson slapped him on the back. "We'll take down the other two."

The three brothers ran in separate directions.

Eying Copper, Zach climbed up on the white picket fence and whistled. His quarter horse left the pack and galloped to him. Keeping an eye out for shooters, he climbed on his friend's back. The ATVs had reached the other end of the pasture.

He turned Copper toward the stables, and they took off. The intruder in black emerged through the open doors. Zach jumped off the horse, landed on top of him, tossed the man's rifle into a stall and then ripped off the mask.

"Larry Sloan." That made sense. He must have learned how to propel out of helicopters in the military. The surprised look on the man's face made Zach smile. "We know everything."

Sloan knocked Zach off of him. They pushed to their feet and took turns throwing punches.

Zach took a hard one to the face and stumbled backward. Rubbing his aching cheek, he glared at the man who had shot out their tire on the switchbacks. "I've had enough of you and your brothers."

"Show me what you've got, cowboy." Larry pulled a switchblade from his pants pocket and danced around like a wrestler. He lunged forward, trying to strike Zach in the chest, but he jumped back. With each swipe of the blade, Zach sidestepped or dove out of the way, then quickly pushed to his feet.

Despite the freezing temperatures, Zach grew hot from exertion. His breathing turned shallow as he evaded another strike. Finally, he spotted a shovel leaning against a stall wall. He ran, grabbed it and turned to find Larry barreling down on him.

With a limited window of opportunity, Zach swung as hard as he could. He hit Larry over the head and knocked him out. "*That's* what I've got. Sleep tight."

Before leaving the barn, Zach grabbed a rope and tied Larry's hands and feet together. Back out in the snow, he spotted his brothers chasing after an ATV. The other vehicle rested on its side, close to Cole's house. *Janel!*

EIGHTEEN

"There's Zach, coming out of the stable." Relief flowed over Janel as she turned the laptop toward Lily. The two women had been sitting on Cole's sofa, watching the ranch's security footage.

"He's alone," Lily pointed out. "He must have taken out the guy who climbed down the helicopter rope."

Janel read aloud the text she sent to Zach. "'What happened to the guy in the stables?'" Seconds later, she shared his answer. "'Tied up. Stay hidden.'"

"I hear sirens. But they're not close." Karla peered out through the living room blinds. "I don't see anyone."

"That doesn't mean no one's there." Janel knew it was something Zach would say. Thinking of him reminded her to pray.

God, I humbly ask for Your protection and guidance in our time of need. Zach says You have a plan, and I've come to believe that is true. You did send him my way. Please keep us all alive and end this nightmare for good. Amen.

"Do you smell smoke?" Armed, Lily rushed toward the dining room, then down the hall.

Drawing in a deep breath, Janel caught the scent, too. Worried, she pushed off the sofa and snatched a gun off the coffee table. "Karla, keep an eye on the front rooms."

Lily opened one door, then another. Janel ran down the hall and around the corner. Clouds of smoke escaped from under the last bedroom door, stealing both her breath and the limited sense of safety she had minutes ago. She reluctantly tapped the brass knob with her finger.

Heart pounding, she whipped around to stop Lily from getting any closer. "The doorknob's hot."

"We have to get out of here!" Lily spun in the opposite direction.

As they ran, Janel asked, "How did we not hear anything? They must have opened a window to get a blaze going that fast."

"The gunshots and ATVs covered up any noise they made." Lily stopped in the living room. "Karla. Fire. Grab a gun and your coat, now!"

"The helicopter pilot had a bird's-eye view. If he saw Zach coming out the front door, he told the others." Karla set aside the laptop and hurried to the dining room.

They set their weapons down on the table and

tugged on the coats they'd left hanging on the backs of wooden chairs.

Janel zipped hers up. "How did they get close to the house without us seeing it on the laptop?"

"They're burglars," Karla reminded her. "They look for cameras and find the blind spots. And they could be out there, waiting for us."

Smoke tendrils slithered into the dining room like a snake.

"That's why we're armed," Lily said before calling her parents to report the fire.

While Zach's sister promised her father they'd head to the main house, Karla removed the tie holding her ponytail and placed it in Janel's palm. "Wear this. They'll think you're me."

"Put your hair back up." She wouldn't let her sister die for her.

"No."

Janel's gaze landed on a rolled-up unread newspaper sitting on the table. She tugged off the rubber band, holding the pages together, and handed it to her sister. In two seconds, they both had their hair secured in ponytails.

The acrid smell of smoke and crackling of the blaze coming from the bedrooms warned them to get out.

"Let's go." Lily opened the door a couple of inches and glanced outside.

Karla grabbed her weapon, then headed out the door after Lily. Her gaze darted about, searching for danger. Janel shoved a gun into her coat pocket to keep her hand warm, hoping she wouldn't need to use it, and followed the others.

They scanned the snow-covered yard and surrounding evergreen trees. The sun's rays filtered through the clouds and reflected off the snow, while a strong breeze whipped around them.

"Won't they burn your parents' house if we go there?" Janel whispered, while glancing over her shoulder to make sure no one followed them.

"We're not staying. My truck's there. If we're fast, we can hightail it away while my brothers keep those guys busy."

Flames engulfed the entire back end of Cole's house. Timbers fell from the burned frame. Janel wished she hadn't been a magnet for trouble. The Walkers were down-to-earth, good, caring people who didn't deserve to suffer through one invasion after another. If only she had turned down Zach's offer to come here.

Lily and Karla had stepped behind a metal shed ahead of her when she heard footfalls in the snow to her left.

"Stop right there," a man's voice commanded.

She froze in place. When she slowly turned her head in his direction, she instantly recognized Sawyer Sloan. He stood roughly a dozen feet away, holding a gun, its barrel pointed at her. Terror exploded in her chest.

"You're coming with me, Karla," he sneered. "I want my money."

He thought she was her sister. If he knew her true identity, he would shoot and kill her. Karla, hidden behind the shed, lifted her finger to her lips, warning her not to speak. They might look alike, but they didn't sound the same.

The wind picked up and whistled through the air vent in the shed. Lily took advantage of the noise to rush forward, spring around the corner and take aim at Sawyer.

Her gun jammed.

Sawyer laughed and shifted the barrel of his gun toward Lily.

A need to protect Zach's sister propelled Janel into action. She dove in front of Lily while trying to rip the weapon out of her coat pocket, but she wasn't fast enough.

A gunshot rang in the air.

Janel felt a sting in her upper body, dropped the gun and fell into the snow. Her mind floated on a haze similar to the one she experienced after hitting her head. She barely recognized the sound of muffled screams. Lying on the cold ground, the flickering image of a man with broad shoulders came into view.

"Zach," she mumbled. She could have been happy with him. "I love you." With that declaration drifting away in the wind, her world turned to darkness.

* * *

After Zach had spotted the smoke above Cole's house, he sprinted to the front door and pounded. No one answered, so he ran around to the kitchen door and found footprints pressed into the snow leading toward the evergreen trees. He followed the trail while keeping an eye out for the Sloan brother who had left the ATV and helmet nearby.

When he heard a man's menacing voice, he circled the trees to come up behind him. That's when he witnessed the beginning of a nightmare. Karla lunged in front of Lily as Sawyer fired his weapon.

Karla slumped to the ground and mumbled something.

Reacting instinctively, Zach whipped his gun from its holster and fired at Sawyer. His body jerked, then another shot rang out—this one coming from Lily's direction—and he fell forward, face down.

After snatching Sawyer's gun and discovering he was unconscious but alive, Zach looked up and found Karla lowering her weapon. Her stance looked practiced, like she'd spent hours in a shooting range. He wasn't surprised; she was an investigator.

Wait a minute, if that's Karla… Janel was the twin lying on the ground. His eyes widened. His mind refused to believe it was possible. That's when he noticed both sisters had their blond locks pulled up into ponytails.

He rushed closer. The fear he might have lost his one true love rose in his chest, urging him into a full sprint.

"Janel!" Karla screamed. "Lily, call 911."

Zach dropped to his knees in front of Janel's motionless body. The welcome sound of sirens finally reached the ranch as he held her wrist and searched for a pulse. It felt faint, but there.

Everything after that moment happened in quick succession. Jackson arrived, announcing that he and Cole had repeatedly shot at Oscar's ATV until it crashed. After throwing a few punches, they managed to take down the third Sloan brother and hand him to the deputies, who also collected Larry from the stables. EMTs worked on both Janel and Sawyer. A short distance away, firefighters valiantly fought the flames while Cole watched.

Zach's emotions were all over the place. He was glad the Sloan brothers had been caught, and he felt horrible about the destruction of Cole's home, but all he could focus on was Janel. His heart ached as he kicked himself for being angry at her earlier. He climbed into the back of the ambulance, determined not to leave her side unless absolutely necessary.

The trip to the hospital was a blur. He alternated between praying and watching her intently, hoping for a sign that she'd wake and be fine. But she didn't. Forcing back tears brought on a splitting headache.

When the ambulance's back door opened, Zach crawled out. He did his best to stay out of the way while watching Janel every second until the doctor told him he had to stay behind. He stared at the closed hospital door, feeling lost and empty. Destroyed.

The bullet had penetrated Janel's body near her shoulder, and she spent hours in surgery.

Lieutenant Yeager ambled into the waiting room, hat in hand. "How's she doing?"

"Hanging in there." Zach shifted position in the uncomfortable chair, wishing someone would tell him she was no longer in danger.

"She's a fighter. I could tell that at the creek."

Zach nodded. "I suppose you want my statement."

"It can wait till morning." Yeager ran his hand through his hair. "Where's her sister?"

"My family practically dragged her to the cafeteria."

"And you didn't go?"

"They've learned to leave me alone when I put my foot down."

"Me, too." The lieutenant smiled. "I wanted you to know Oscar Sloan is already talking. He's been to prison before and knows the advantages of cooperation."

"I hope they all plead out. Janel's suffered enough already. She doesn't need the hassle of a trial…if she makes it through surgery."

"Don't go there. She will. And then her life can go back to normal. The Sloan brothers are no longer a threat, and both her and her sister have cleared their names where the gallery burglary is concerned. Karla still needs a competent lawyer. She broke a few laws while proving their innocence."

Zach knew he was referring to the break-in at the hotel where Karla planted the recording device, then her transferring the ill-gotten gains to the insurance company. "I'll tell her."

The surgeon stepped into the waiting room, his mask dangling from one ear, and called out for the family of Janel Newman.

Zach, fearing the worst, tried to read his face as he walked up to him. "Doc, how is she?"

"The surgery went well. You can see her when she wakes up." The surgeon described the medical aspects of her condition, but Zach couldn't get past the fact she was alive and he could see her soon.

The seconds seemed to tick by even slower after the doctor and lieutenant left. He called Karla to share the good news. She returned shortly with

Lily and his parents. They had stopped by the gift shop on their way back.

"We bought candy and games for Janel." Karla lifted a purse-type bag made from quilted material.

"That was thoughtful." Maybe he should have picked up something for her.

His mother gave him a hug and whispered, "All Janel needs is you. Don't let this one get away."

"I won't." Thinking about how close he came to losing her, through both his stubbornness and the shooting, took his breath away. He tightened his grip on the brim of his Stetson. "I'm going to stay here. You should take Dad and Lily home."

After they left, he passed on Yeager's suggestion of getting a good lawyer.

"With what?" Karla answered. "I'm currently unemployed."

"Fired?"

She nodded. "You know, when Janel opened the gallery, she asked me if I wanted to be her business partner. If I sell my house, I could pay back her loan, save Mom's paintings from the bank and hire that lawyer."

"If only you had thought of that before meeting Sawyer Sloan." He sent her a half smile.

"If only…" She scrubbed her face with the palms of her hands. "I do love my sister and never dreamed that anything like this would happen."

He believed that about her. "Everything will work out. God has a plan."

After a brief frown, the lines on Karla's forehead disappeared and her shoulders relaxed. "Maybe it's time I went to church again."

"You have a ride anytime you need one." He knew Janel would be pleased.

Karla slapped her thigh. "That's another thing I need. A new car. Mine blew up."

Charlene arrived, carrying a vase filled with yellow roses, minutes after a nurse told them Janel was now awake but would be groggy. Karla filled her in on what happened at the ranch as they headed to the assigned room together.

Not willing to wait any longer, Zach stepped inside ahead of the others. Janel opened her eyes, and the weight of the world lifted off his shoulders. With emotions threatening to choke him, he cleared his throat and moved closer to the bed. "Hi, there. You gave us all a scare."

"Sorry." She closed her lids, then opened them again. "You know me. I'll do anything to get out of running another festival."

He chuckled. "And here I was thinking we could cochair the next one."

She squeezed his hand, then fell asleep again. He remained at her side, watching her, thanking God for sparing her life.

The next time she woke, Karla spoke to her, then Charlene. "Robert sends his best."

"Thank him for me." Janel was more alert, more like herself. When Zach kissed her forehead, the others left the room, giving them privacy.

He pushed stray strands of hair away from her face. "I thought I lost you forever."

"Does this mean you're not mad at me anymore?" Her voice was faint, but her words packed a powerful punch.

Regret flashed through him. "I was a fool. I shouldn't have compared you to my ex. You're not at all alike. Your words and actions prove you're a good, caring woman. And you protect your family the way I do."

Janel placed her hand on top of his. "I *should have* kept comparing you to my ex. You two are so different. The truth is, there were signs Todd was no good. I just didn't want to admit it. With all the work at my gallery and then my mother's cancer, it was easier to have a boyfriend who was gone most of the time, but still there when I wanted to call him."

"Do you still want a long-distance boyfriend?"

"No. I want you, Zach Walker."

"I love you." He placed a tender kiss on her lips.

"I love you, too." Her gaze held his. Their connection was undeniable.

The door opened, and Cole poked his head inside, looking sheepish. "Sorry to interrupt, but

Zach, there is someone you need to meet. It's important."

He placed another kiss on her forehead. "I'll be back shortly."

When he left the room, Karla and Charlene walked back inside. She'd be in good hands while he was away.

"What's this all about?" Zach asked his brother, admittedly exhausted and wishing he could stay with Janel.

"I received a phone call from a guy who works at the airport. He thinks he knows the pilot who was flying Larry Sloan around. He's on his way over."

"I almost forgot about him." Zach picked up his pace. They had to wait in the parking lot for ten minutes before a man in his late forties pulled up in a white work van.

"You Detective Walker?"

Cole lifted his hand. "I am. This is Deputy Walker."

"Like I said on the phone, my friend told me about a blue helicopter being involved in some shootings. He thought I might know more about it."

"Why would you?" Cole asked.

"I repair helicopters."

Now he had Zach's interest. "I'm assuming you do, or you wouldn't be here."

"I got a call from a pilot who flies for a real es-

tate developer. The landing skid on his blue helicopter was bent, like maybe someone shot at it.
He was real nervous. Said it had to be fixed before the weekend. His boss wants a flight back
from Phoenix."

Zach tried to act nonchalant while his nerves
twitched with anticipation. "Who's this pilot?"

"Robert Matthews."

Charlene's boyfriend. Zach was thunderstruck.
The enemy was sitting in their camp the entire
time. This explained how the Sloan brothers knew
Janel's alarm code. He watched his girlfriend
enter it during one of their trips to the gallery.

The man glanced over his shoulder. "I have to
get back to work. Don't tell anyone I gave you
a name. I want to live long enough to retire one
day." With that, he drove away.

Zach turned to his brother. "How does a guy
with no record end up flying for the Sloans?"

Cole shook his head. "We should have checked
to see if Matthews's path crossed Larry Sloan's
during their military days. I'll get an address and
find out what he drives."

"No need." Zach's ire returned as he pointed
to a distinctive green Mercedes-Benz parked two
rows away. "He's here. And he knows Karla can
access millions of dollars."

Afraid his universe might crumble, Zach ran
inside the hospital, hoping he wasn't too late.

NINETEEN

"How lovely. Thank you." Janel admired the crystal vase filled with yellow roses that Charlene placed on a small round table in front of the window.

"They brighten up the room, don't you think?" Charlene moved to the foot of the hospital bed as Janel nodded her agreement.

"Here's something else guaranteed to put a smile on your face." Karla dug through a quilted bag, then handed Janel a yellow pen with a cartoon head on the end. "You used to have one just like it."

The mop of blue hair and goofy grin on the head made Janel chuckle. "Ah, I did, and if I remember right, you broke it."

Karla pointed to herself, feigning innocence before admitting, "I might have accidentally stepped on it."

"As long as it was accidental," Janel teased as she gestured to the bag she'd never seen before. "What else is in there?"

"Red licorice and puzzle books." Karla placed her gifts on the over-the-bed table next to a plastic water pitcher. Her expression suddenly turned serious. "I'm so relieved the surgery went well. I can't lose you."

Touched, Janel placed her hand over her heart. Before she could say anything, the door burst open.

Charlene's boyfriend rushed into the room. His wild eyes, like those of a trapped animal, made the hair on Janel's neck stand on end.

"Robert! You're back." Charlene lifted her hands to hug him until he pulled a gun out from beneath his coat. Her jaw dropped open, and she backed away from him.

Janel froze as she stared at the barrel of his weapon. The bandages covering her bullet wound grew heavier as the memory of being shot replayed in her mind.

He pointed the gun at Karla. "You're going to give me that five million dollars."

No! God, please don't let anything happen to my sister. Janel had to distract him. "You were in on the burglary. You fed the Sloans information, like the fact we were staying at the ranch and every place we said we were headed to, didn't you?"

"Stop stalling. Your boyfriend is outside talking to his brother. He's not coming back anytime soon." He waved the gun around, and Janel sucked in a breath. When she glanced at the call button, his intense glare bore into her. "Don't even think about it. If a nurse shows up, I'll shoot."

Karla lifted her hands, palms out. "I'll give you the money."

"Wait a minute." Charlene's eyes grew wide with anger as she fisted her hands at her side. "Did you date me to get the alarm code?"

"What of it?"

His attitude made Charlene's face turn red.

"How do you even know the Sloans?" Janel asked, feeling the need to step in between her assistant manager and Robert—verbally, if not physically.

"Larry and I have been friends since we were kids." He pointed the gun at Karla again. "Money. I have an account I want it transferred into."

"That's all you have to say?" Charlene glared at him.

"You should be thanking me," he blurted, his patience spent. "I'm teaching you a valuable lesson. Stop being so gullible." He pointed the gun directly at Charlene. "Enough talking!"

Janel gritted her teeth. The guy was so jumpy he might accidentally shoot someone. He wasn't acting like a man who had military training. Was his friend Larry the type to name accomplices for a lighter sentence? Is that what had Robert so desperate to get his hands on the money to leave town that he would risk coming to the hospital with law enforcement officers on the property?

The door, set back in a six-foot-long hallway, inched open.

Janel's pulse skipped a beat.

Zach poked his head into the room. He made eye contact with Janel and held his finger to his lips. Robert had his back to him, and a good dozen feet separated them.

Karla's gaze flitted about the room, landing on Zach at least once. She lifted the quilted bag off the table and stepped back toward the wall. "I need my phone to transfer the money."

Was her sister trying to lure Robert away from the hospital bed? Trying once more to keep Janel out of danger? If so, her plan wasn't working. He hadn't budged an inch.

If Zach tried to shoot him, he could hit Janel by mistake.

Janel fingered the pen in her right hand, the uninjured side of her body. What they needed was a distraction that would allow Zach to rush in and subdue Robert.

When Robert reached into his coat pocket for a slip of paper and handed it to Karla, Janel threw her pen as hard and fast as she could. The cartoon head smacked against the window.

Robert spun around and shot. The sound of breaking window glass held his attention for at least two seconds. Long enough for Karla to extend her foot out in front of him and push hard.

Zach exploded into the room, lunged on top of him and ripped the gun from his hand as they fell to the floor.

Cole opened the door, took in the sight and rushed over to take the weapon. He passed a set of handcuffs to his brother.

"Robert Matthews, you're under arrest." Zach clamped the cuffs around the man's wrists.

Janel finally released the pent-up breath she'd been holding.

"You creep!" Charlene snatched the vase from the small wooden table and dumped the water and roses over Robert's head.

Cole grabbed the crystal vase from her hands. "Okay, that's enough."

She screamed at her now ex-boyfriend. "That's what you get for using defenseless women."

Zach pulled Robert up off the floor and chuckled. "There is nothing defenseless about any of you." He sent Janel a loving smile. "Especially you."

EPILOGUE

Six months later, Janel sat in the gallery's new café area, watching her sister test the espresso machine. "Make mine a white chocolate."

"You got it," Karla said, grinning from ear to ear. She had sold her house in Scottsdale the first week it was on the market. That allowed her to invest enough money into the gallery to pay back the bank loan and divide the education room into two areas. The café being one of them. They offered coffee, hot chocolate, tea, milk and pastries. And while customers sat at stylish bistro tables, they could watch an artist in residence through a glass wall. Today, their painter, a cowboy with good manners and deep blue eyes, was hard at work in the well-lit studio.

Janel's mood had lifted since the Sloan brothers and Robert signed plea bargains and were safely behind bars. Although she felt badly for Sawyer's son. The lieutenant learned the boy was doing much better after starting his medical treatments, but he would surely miss his father. She would keep him in her prayers.

She sipped her mocha and gave her sister a thumbs-up. "This is better than the café down the street. We should charge fifty cents less to drive traffic this way."

"The best part is no other gallery around here serves food or coffee." Karla slipped into the chair opposite hers. "Sedona Imagined is no longer a threat."

"Do you miss working as an investigator?"

"I thought I would, but I don't. Getting fired was the best thing that could have happened for the both of us." Karla scanned the room with the expression of a proud parent.

Janel smiled as she lifted the warm cup to her lips.

"It's time for me to unlock the front door." Karla marched off, leaving Janel to her thoughts.

Charlene popped her head inside the room. "I'm off to the post office."

"We need more mailing cylinders." Janel waved goodbye, reflecting on how they had made the right decision, giving Charlene a pay raise and putting her in charge of online sales. She had a knack for internet commerce. She was also renting rooms to the sisters while their mother's house was being rebuilt. This time, the insurance company wasn't giving them any trouble.

Janel recognized the voice floating in from the

showroom. Her heart filled with joy as she rushed into the main area. She found Zach looking up at the bright swirls of color on *Sun Setting on Rocks*.

"Hi." Was it her imagination, or was he even more handsome than the day she met him?

"Hi, yourself." He reached out his hand, pulling her to his side. "Your mother's painting looks much better here than on a cold backyard studio easel."

"My mom believed all art should be displayed for the public to enjoy. That's why she wanted me to open my gallery."

He squeezed her hand, held it up to his lips and kissed her fingers. "You look happy."

"I was thinking about what you said. God sometimes shakes things up so we'll choose a new path. I think He threw me off my old one." She chuckled. "But life is much better, and not just for me. Karla is an exceptional business partner."

"Only because you bounce ideas off each other," Zach clarified. "Don't underestimate what you bring to the table."

She felt a blush heat her cheeks. "We work well together. Anyway, I was going over the books this morning. The gallery is now officially out of the red."

"That's wonderful."

"If sales keep up, we'll have a record year." She placed her hand on his strong jawline, taking in the woodsy scent of his cologne. "You get some of the credit for our success. You introduced me to your social media influencer. Sarah's a real go-getter."

"That she is." His smile reached his dark brown eyes. "I signed a contract with a new resort this morning while you were balancing your books. You know, I was exaggerating when I asked Sarah if she could make Walker Ranch as famous as the O.K. Corral, but she might just reach that goal as long as Hollywood doesn't make another Wyatt Earp movie within the next few years. Lily is coming up with a speech to give tourists on hayrides, telling them where the shoot-outs happened and what blew up."

"Let's not forget your uncle. The cabin he gave your mother will go a long way in rebuilding your family's business."

"True. No more protecting witnesses on the ranch means no more gunfights." He planted a kiss on her forehead. "No more looking over our shoulders for gunmen. And no more resort managers pulling their business."

"Should we celebrate our mutual success and brighter future?"

"Wonderful idea." He released her hand and then reached into his jeans pocket. "I was going to do this tonight, but standing here, beneath your mother's painting, feels right. You went through so much to save this place, the paintings, your life, your sister's life, and prove your innocence.

That struggle brought us closer together—forever, I hope."

She tried to peek at what he held, but he gripped it tightly. Was he going to…?

He lowered to one knee, and her heart leaped in her chest.

Yes, yes, a million times yes. She forced herself to remain silent until he popped the question.

"Janel, love of my life, will you marry me?" Zach held out a sparkling diamond ring. "I want to wake up beside you every morning and grow old with you by my side."

"Yes, I will marry you. The sooner the better."

Grinning, he placed the ring on her finger. A perfect fit.

While the magnitude of this moment swept over her, he stood and pulled her into his arms. "I love you, Janel Newman."

She gazed into the eyes of the man who had made all her dreams come true. "And I love you, Zach Walker. Now kiss me."

* * * * *

*If you liked this story from Tina Wheeler,
check out her previous
Love Inspired Suspense books,*

Ranch Under Fire
Ranch Showdown

*Available now from Love Inspired Suspense!
Find more great reads at
www.LoveInspired.com.*

Dear Reader,

I hope you enjoyed this third book in the Red Rock Country series. Zach and Janel have huge hearts, making them two of my favorite characters. They deserved their happily ever after, but they had to travel a dangerous road to get there.

When Janel admits she feels like God has abandoned her, Zach shares his belief that He sometimes shakes us out of our comfort zone, so we'll choose an alternative path to travel. I have found this to be true several times in my life. When I look back on troubling times, I can see where one event led to another, which eventually led to great blessings. God truly has a plan for us.

I love hearing from readers! You can contact me through my website www.authortinawheeler. com. While you're there, I hope you'll sign up for my newsletter for behind-the-scenes news and giveaway opportunities.

Blessings,
Tina

   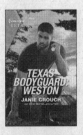